Wednesday Tupperware

GW00853374

T.A.GILBERT

A Collection of Short Stories
and Short Shorts

Imogen,

I hope you enjoy!

Love

Tracy x.

For the love of my sister,
the wisdom of my mother and,
the memory of my father.

CONTENTS

Wednesday Night Tupperware

'Come on Abi, move it. We're gonna be late.'

Mum's standing at the door of our flat. She's got that rotten light blue holdall, bulging with hard corners, at her feet.

'I'm nearly ready Mum.'

'Well get a shifty on, I don't want to be late. Those rich cows from the Wellington Estate are going to be there tonight.'

If only she would stop talking to me I could get this snood on properly. Everyone is wearing these hat-come-scarves; they are the must have item of 1987. The magazine open on my bed has a picture of Carol Decker smiling at me from the pages, perfect burnt orange snood arranged under her curly flame red hair. I have been trying to do this for at least ten minutes; trying to turn myself into a number one pop artist rather than the Michelin Man. I give it one more tug and leave the bedroom.

People on the bus tut as my mother pulls the huge bag through the aisle, and plonks it onto a seat. She moves into the row in front and signals to me to sit next to it, as always. I sit down and push the bag with one shoulder. I don't really want to associate myself with it, but even more I don't want it to crash to the floor. So I look after it, just as she knows I will.

We're on our way to the Wellington Estate; a new red brick group of flats. They're not council, they're a co-op which is much more posh than council because people have to vote to let you in. Carol, who used to live next door but one, left our flats last year and moved to Armsworth House the other co-op flats in the Walworth Road. At first she came back every Thursday to go to

1

Bingo with Mum and Diane, but she hasn't been for ages and Mum says she's forgotten where she came from.

The bus lurches forward and for a second I think we're in for a catastrophe. I can see it all in my mind; juice jugs and lunch boxes rolling around under the seats, my mother pointing a finger from a hand still crossed under her arm at the escapees, and me groping around on the floor of the bus trying to recapture them all. But, my reflexes are good and my arm swings out just in time, slapping the bag back onto the seat. We start to chug through roads full of traffic, past shops where owners are taking in the wares that have filled the pavement. Faded awnings announce, "Everything for a Pound", and "Bargain Electrical Goods – Nearly New". When the bus conductor comes, Mum asks for one and a half and throws her head backwards at me without looking. He peers at me and repeats the word half, through a crooked smile. I'm glad of his look, he thinks I'm older. I'm loving this snood.

'Yes half. She's eleven.'

He stands there looking between me and Mum.

'What do you want, her birth certificate?' she snaps as she glares into his face.

He takes the money that she pushes towards him and rings two tickets through. She doesn't talk to me until we get off.

At the Wellington Estate, the floor of Joyce's maisonette is full of plastic containers, bright coloured bowls and beakers with little plastic lids, that I know leak. Mum made me try one and it ruined my history homework. The women sit squashed onto the sofa, their shoulders rounded forward, holding glasses filled to the brim of warm white wine. Some are on dining room chairs and a couple are sat on a bean bag from one of the kids' bedrooms. They finish their game of farmyard bingo. Mum calls it an ice-breaker, but I can never believe that grown up women get so excited and laugh so hard at themselves making cow, sheep and cockerel noises. When they win a *sauce grabber*, a very long handled spoon for getting the last bit of tomato sauce out of the bottle, they clap like Mum has given them a hundred pounds.

Now she's ready to start demonstrating the Tupperware. She takes a green box, a bit bigger than a lunch box, from behind her and lays it in front of her knees.

'Now ladies,' she says like she's on a market stall. 'I can't make anything you buy any fresher, but I can help you keep what you buy fresher for longer.'

They ooh and ahh and watch as she turns the box around and takes the little slotted divider out, followed by what looks like a false floor. She always starts with this one.

'And hey presto,' she tells them. 'Fresher salad.'

'Now ladies, can anyone guess what the most important thing is when using the wonderful Mega Salad Saver?'

A woman puts up her hand, like she knows the capital city of Norway or the value of X.

'Yep, Nora isn't it?' Mum says to her.

The woman nods.

'Nora, what do you think is the most important thing?'

'That you burp it,' says Nora.

Mum tilts her head sideways and looks at Nora, like she's a five year old. 'Now,' she says. 'You may have been to places where these things get burped, but the Tupperware I sell, well it's a bit more classy than that. So Nora, darling, the most important thing to do when using the Mega Salad Saver is to.................,' she pauses and they all lean forward. 'The most important thing is, to .... whisper it.' She pushes the lid down and then lifts one corner to let the air escape. 'Hey presto,' she repeats, 'fresher salad.'

Mum's been selling Tupperware for over a year now; she won part time agent of the quarter last month. I went with her to the meeting near Heathrow. It took us ages to get there on the tube and she was moaning tons about having to travel so far west; until she won. She's putting money away so that we can all go to my cousin's wedding in Spain this summer. When we first got the invite Dad said we couldn't go, there were other things to spend our money on. But Mum said we weren't going to be outcasts at her own niece's wedding and so she started selling Tupperware in the evening. Dad said fair enough.

I do the packing up, while Mum fills out orders and takes everyone's money. A really big woman is ordering two salad savers and a lettuce dryer. Mum tells her that she has lost a stone since she started selling Tupperware. She tells her that the whole family eats more vegetables and that we don't have anything that

3

she hasn't cooked herself, because now she uses the meal freezing boxes. The woman adds a multi-pack of containers to her order and agrees to host a party herself. I have got everything back into the big blue bag. I'm expert at this now and I can do it in record time. I am also expert at making sure nothing disappears. There was once or twice in the beginning when someone had sticky fingers and we went home with a gap in the bag and a scowl on Mum's face.

The bus comes quickly and the ride home seems to whiz by. Mum is in a good mood, she promises me that I can choose something from the market on Saturday. I visualize a new snood; electric blue maybe.

I like Wednesday night Tupperware best. Mum has this arrangement where she goes to a big house in Brixton. It's got four storeys; orange light glows from the window in the basement kitchen. I've never been inside. On Wednesdays I leave Mum at the bus stop across the road. They don't like having children in the house, and so I run to the little cinema across the street and she goes into the big house. Mum says the people are upper class. They have loads of friends; different ones come every week and spend money. If I was that rich, I wouldn't buy Tupperware. I'd have a maid who went shopping every day and cooked amazing dinners, with champagne. I wouldn't be worried about getting the last drop of sauce out of a bottle. We don't tell Dad about the big house. Mum says he has a chip on his shoulder when it comes to money and he'd get upset. So it's our secret.

Once or twice the film has finished early and I have knocked on the door to collect Mum. It can take ages to get anyone to answer and it's usually Mum. Once she looked really red in the face. They make her run around all the time. They won't let her take the big bag up to the top of the house where they have a room for entertaining, so she has to keep trudging up and down the stairs. I have never seen Vivian, who Mum calls the woman of the house. I saw her husband once; he stood at the end of the hallway as Mum whipped on her coat and pulled the Tupperware bag out of the door. He wouldn't look at me properly. He was as red as Mum. Vivien must make him run around as well.

Tonight, as I'm half way through the film I can sense someone walking about. I don't realise it's Mum until I hear people next to me huffing and puffing and I look around and spot her in the aisle. She grabs my arm and tells me we have to leave straight away. She looks like she's been crying, but when I ask what's wrong she says she's just tired. She puts an arm around me as we walk and keeps kissing my head. Her lipstick has come off; a dark pink stain is stuck to the rim of her lips and a faint grey trail of mascara lines her cheek. I want to tell her how much I love her and how I don't want her to be alone in that big house anymore, with those posh people pushing her around. She catches me looking at her and tries to smile, but it comes out all wonky.

She sits next to the bag on the bus on the way home and tells me to sit in front of her. I can hear her sniffing but every time I look around she jabs me in the shoulder and tells me to turn back. We don't go straight home from the bus stop; she heads towards the building site a few roads away. I follow her, trotting to stay in step. When we get to the site, she strides up to a big yellow skip, puts the blue bag on the floor and unzips it. She starts to throw the boxes, cups and plastic cutlery into the skip.

'What are you doing Mum?' I ask.

'I'm getting rid. This is no way to change your life.' She is crying now. She doesn't try to hide it and the tears flow down her face.

'What did they do to you Mum?' I ask scared and starting to cry myself.

'Nothing that I didn't do to myself,' she sobs.

'What about the wedding? How will we get the money?' I don't care about the wedding, but I don't know what else to say.

She gulps and coughs, like a drink has gone down the wrong way. She throws the last piece of plastic into the skip and then holds my face in her hands.

'What's a wedding?' She strokes my cheeks with her thumbs. I don't move. 'People making promises they can't keep.'

I let her hug me tightly for what feels like ages and then she takes my hand and leads me home, the empty bag, hanging like a flag without wind from her fingers.

Touch

The second time they had dinner she made it clear that she wanted him to touch her.

She wanted him to touch her in the morning, as soon as he awoke, before he had a chance to stretch the night from his muscles or wet the dryness of his mouth. She wanted him to touch her as he reached past her in the bedroom, stretching up and over her to pick clothes from the wardrobe. She wanted him to touch her as he pushed the chair under her before they ate. His fingers were expected to find her shoulder, or the hollow at the top of her spine, before words connected them. Even when they were in the tranquil paradise of his garden, each tending separate flower beds, he daren't simply call her name; he had to go to her.

She watched him in his workshop where he was patient with his talent. She noted the occasional smile that spread to his eyes, as he quietly celebrated the marriage of his beautiful ideas, nurturing his chisel through the hunks of oak at his feet. On these days she would stand behind him, waiting. She knew that when he sensed her he would stop and stand and touch her. He hadn't found her desire easy at first. Early attempts were clumsy; fumbled grabs and squeezes that were just a little too tight. At times he'd even pushed her off balance, though he was convinced the caress was weightless.

He was confused for a while, sometimes touching her too intimately, making her close her eyes and wince at the contact. He wasn't aware that early on he was using vessels to meet her; a glass of wine, a pencil, passing her a book. He read instruction in the flick of her eyes and would bring her body to the objects, wrap her fingers around a stem, form her hands as if in prayer to accept a book. He learned quickly, being rewarded with the tiniest of smiles and minute upward glances.

Yet sometimes she could be so magnificently spiteful. It was all that he could do but sit and watch, mesmerised, as she lashed out, twisting words, and spitting venom. Then, once the screaming subsided, he would rise and go to her, sooth and calm her, pull her close and hold her until, at last, she was still and silent. When moments later she smiled, seemingly recovered, he couldn't help but wonder if it had all been a means to this end.

Soon every breath was for her.

She gave herself to him.

More and more often they spent days wrapped up in each other, ignoring everything else. It became a feast of physical intimacy, each dining on every detail of the other. Eventually they would emerge into the open air, filling their lungs with the outside, better practised at maintaining the sticky bond between them.

Now he could reach her in a second, deftly moving her hair from her face before it could fall into her eyes, protecting her hand from the cold the second she removed it from a glove.

After some time she moved into his flat. He warmed the walls with shades of chocolate, vanilla and pale pink; hung textured prints and scattered cushions. She giggled with delight as she hugged and breathed in the soft warm gifts of jumpers, rugs and throws. Her smiles illuminated his flat and turned it into their home.

He started to take her into his workshop, draping rich, dark, velvety pashminas over boxes. Folds of material blocked out portions of light so that he had to move his bench to see his work. As he shut the door her perfume lingered as the breeze caught and lifted the sail of her. Dust stuck to the material with incredible determination and she would rise with anger when her things got ruined, but he would touch her and bring her peace. He wanted to wrap her in the clothes from the workshop, feel the needles of the chippings on her as he held her, watch the light smears of the dust try to move as he felt her. She told him she wanted to feel his skin on hers, experience a pure touch, and he gave it to her, needing to feel the rush of his blood as she rewarded his fingers.

On Sundays they lay in bed as he stroked her, drawing shapes over her, worshipping her. On this day she held his hand, pressing his palm gently into her flesh and then moving it, back and forth, over the faint hill of her belly. He looked down to see shadows bouncing off her skin and felt the pull of her eyes. He tried to move his hand to her face without looking at her, but she held it firmly on her stomach and with her other hand turned his face to hers. He felt strange, and noticed for the first time the colours dancing in her irises. He held her gaze and waited for her to speak. But she didn't. He looked back down to his hand and started to move it under hers, gradually being granted more liberty. He felt for her heart, but couldn't read its regularity.

He was still looking at his hand when she suddenly moved and slithered from under him. She slid out of bed, out into the hall and he heard her go into to the bathroom and lock the door.

He was sitting on the floor playing with the collar of her bathrobe when she came out and looked down at him. He reached out and found her calf, slid his hand up to the back of her knee and drew her leg to his face. He brushed his cheek over the top of her shin and then kissed it. Finally, she slipped down the wall to meet him on the floor and whispered through the air between them that it wouldn't be just the two of them for much longer.

The first things he couldn't touch were her breasts. They quickly became full and sore. Next, as her waist began to thicken, she told him she didn't want to be held. She no longer felt attractive and didn't want him to experience her like this. He tried to focus on the parts of her body that were seemingly unchanged. He tried to hold her face in his hands; tried to massage the tightness out of her shoulders and ease away the tension at her temples.

As she grew he tried to connect with his child, gently touching his fingertips on her bump as she slept, but he always seemed to wake her.

With eight weeks before the new life would breathe their atmosphere she told him she didn't have enough love for both of them. She told him she didn't have enough skin to meet both their demands. She said he was a man who needed physical assurance and that motherhood would mean her caresses would be employed in sustaining her child.

Two weeks before he was due to hold his child, she left.

No Uncle

I knock twice on the door. Each time the thick knot of iron hits the plate my stomach muscles contract. I take a breath and stand back against the balcony wall. Boys in baggy tracksuit bottoms and bright coloured trainers play football in the square below. A car alarm starts but I saw the football hit the bonnet, and so I don't jump.

The envelope in my hand feels damp. It is my reluctant duty.

The door opens slowly and he is there, smaller and paler; his skin is the colour of cheap chocolate. His eyes have yellowed. His gold tooth hangs in his mouth.

He smiles and backs away, silently inviting me to enter.

We sit facing each other in a small room that smells of stale beer and sweat. The arm of his chair is worn. I smile. As a kid, I watched him bouncing keys of posh cars, up and down, on the arm of our sofa. Mum seethed until Dad asked his brother to stop.

'Hello child,' he whispers.

I cannot speak. My mouth is dry and my teeth are stuck to my lips. I want to hand him the ticket, pack for him and leave.

He tries again.

'Hello Elston,' I say.

He winces. 'No uncle?' he asks.

'No uncle,' I say. 'Just Elston.'

He looks at the package on my lap, then at the floor.

His feet are dry and cracked in his slippers. They move, as I stand up proffering my package. He bows, still sitting in his faded chair.

I show myself out.

The game of football continues as I cross the gravel. A ball arcs and bounces off the roof of my Peugeot. I feel the boys' stillness as they wait for the alarm.

Nothing.

All is quiet.

Sorted!

Dark's what I see a lot of, stood in a doorway five nights a week, watching people come in and helping others on their way out. I know every shop window next to this bar. There's Woolies, Old Jacob's the pawnbroker, and the Potato House; believe me that gets a bit lively when this place shuts.

Tonight, I'm going out myself and I'm in the cab, which smells of dodgy pine forest and bad hygiene, but I'm warm and my feet are off the floor. Doing this job, you have to get out every now and again or you'd never see the inside of anywhere. So, I booked my midnight finish and I'm on my way to pick up the girlfriend. I popped into the cab office earlier and got my order in so that I could get away bang on twelve. Twelve came and I ended up having a touch of trouble with a suit over this car. I could tell him and his mates were going to give me gip from the way they all waltzed down the street, towards the bar. It gets my goat up thinking about it, so I'll leave telling you the rest until later.

I've been a bouncer for six years. 'Course I've done other stuff. I did all right at school. I wasn't a swot but I wasn't thick either. I did O'levels in Maths and English and then CSEs in everything else. Mr Edwards was our English teacher. Weird fella, he had a lick of hair that stuck out the top of his head like a chicken's comb, and he wore striped jumpers that were always a bit too tight, but he was a good sport. Me and my mate Jack locked him in a cupboard once. He was teaching us about this book, trying to get us to tell him how we thought this bloke, whose brother was a bit dim, felt. The girls were getting right into it. I remember one of them shoving her hand up in the air, balancing on the edge of her seat, almost exploding.

'Yes Ruth,' Mr Edwards said.

'He feels protective,' Ruth spat out.

Then Jack started laughing like a lunatic; he always did that.

'Have you got something to add, Jack?' Mr Edwards asked.

'Yeah. I reckon he's pissed off having a numbnuts for a brother.'

Well, we all cracked up and Mr Edwards told us that was it. He said we could all sit there whilst he read James Joyce. He walked into one of the store cupboards to get his book, and me and Jack were up like lightning, and we locked him in. The pips went ten minutes later, and I let him out because I kind of liked him. He came out, a bit red, but he didn't go ape shit; he laughed, a real belly laugh. Of course we all got detention for a week, but the bloke laughed. So I kept on with English, and the funny thing is what he told me stuck. He said, everyone should love words. And I do. You see I developed this habit; I sort of collect them. I look them up in this big old dictionary I've got indoors. You can find all sorts in it. Did you know that there's a single word that means throwing someone out of a window? 'DEFENESTRATION'. How about that? Now that's clever.

When I left school, my uncle got me a job in the Post Office. It was okay money, but boring. I stayed because a few lads off the estate worked there and we used to have a laugh. My heart was never in it, but I always got my work done, not like some of the lazy gits there. They probably did me a favour when they sacked me. I reckon you could get used to doing that job every day, and then one morning wake up fifty years old and realise you've spent your whole life putting other people's mail into the right sack. Mind you, I wasn't happy when they gave me the push, just for being a bit late.

After that I did bits and pieces for a while. I even worked in the warehouse at Marks and Spencer's. Now my mum loved that one. There was a staff shop where everything was cheap and she used to give me a list as long as your arm. I used to look a right idiot walking through the estate of an evening with big bags of shopping. There was one Easter, when she told me to buy whatever poultry I could for twenty quid, so I bought the usual chicken and then I spotted this massive goose. I couldn't resist it. I lugged that thing back on the bus; it got heavier and heavier as I made my way home. If I'd have swung it at anyone, I'd have killed them. By the time I'd walked from the bus stop and got to the estate, the handles of the plastic bag had almost snapped and I had deep red marks in my fingers. In the lift, I held that bag like a child to my chest, the rest of the shopping digging into my arms. Mum was chuffed when she saw it, although she had to phone my nan and ask how to cook it. It was gorgeous. I've never had it since, but I can still taste it. You know, thinking about it, I don't think we ever ate so good as when I worked in that warehouse.

When Marks's came to an end I thought about doing The Knowledge to get my cabbie's badge. I know London like the back of my hand, I've got a half decent memory and setting my own hours would be right up my street. But to tell you the truth I didn't think I'd be able to stomach it, all those people getting in my cab all day, not having a clue about where they're going. It would have wound me right up.

I could never work in an office, not me. Not like the prats that come into Whispers on a Thursday and Friday night. Half the blokes look like their suits are trying to strangle them, all up tight and with a right smell under their noses. It's like this group of suits that turned up earlier tonight; the ones I had the trouble with. Three blokes and a couple of girls. They weren't regulars or anything but they walked in like they owned the place, smiling at me because they wanted to get in. It was early, no queue, or I would have had a bit of fun with them and made them hang about for a bit. One of them tapped me on the arm and said, 'Evening my friend', as he walked past. Patronizing git! They think I'm low life just because I'm a bouncer. It does my head in. They don't know anything about me and I'm not their friend. I know loads of stuff they don't. It's like my words; I don't remember all the ones I look up, but I still make an effort and I'll never stop learning.

You can't get too bothered by the suits doing this job. My approach is to just watch them; they're entertainment most of the time, like watching a television show. Every time we open the door to let people in, you can see right into the bar; loads of little stories going on among the chrome and black leather. Some of them never move from the place they buy their first pint. They start off civilised, drinking nicely, loads of chat. Couple of hours later they're all over the place. Their smart suits and their wedding rings forgotten. Into oblivion, and out of marriage. It's just like the group I was telling you about. They'd hardly noticed I was breathing the same air as them once they'd walked through the door, but a couple of hours later they want my help. The biggest bloke, a right ugly fella with a nose Barry Manilow would be proud of, comes up to me, slurring.

'I've had my laptop stolen,' he says as though I'm Paul Daniels and can make it reappear.

'So where did you last see it?' I ask him.

He spins around, like a Jack Russell chasing its tail, and ends up facing me again. 'Over there,' he says pointing to the side of us.

'What by the Ladies' toilets?' I ask patiently.

'I didn't go in the Ladies' toilets.'

'No, I know mate. Where did you leave your laptop?'

He stands and smiles at me. He's getting a few laughs from his mates and so he plays the clown for a bit, and I just stare at him.

I'm not surprised when I finally manage to get him to tell me what happened. Him and his mates had taken the girls to the dance floor and left it under their coats by the bar. Now, I don't care how many letters you've got after your name, but you have to be pretty damn stupid to leave something worth hundreds of pounds by a bar while you have a boogie. All you can do is take their names and addresses and tell them to report it to the police. They're always convinced there's something else you can do; like what, shut all the doors and strip search everyone?

Saturday nights are different. It's mainly locals and that's when I really enjoy this job. I know most people who come to Whispers at the weekend. Half my mates do. Alfie and Jack haven't missed a Saturday night in about two years. Even if they go somewhere else first, they always end up propping up the bar at last orders. And you don't have to look to find them. You can smell Alfie; he likes a cigar. We call him Mr De Niro, and if you tap him on the back at the right moment he chokes on the thing and ends up spluttering like an eighty year old. Even on the night of Jack's wedding we ended up down there. We were all ushers and when the do in the Windmill finished at one, we put all the girls in cabs home and went down to Whispers. What a laugh. The whole lot of us all trussed up in these penguin suits, dancing our heads off.

Jack's nickname is Pele, on account of the fact he could have been a professional footballer. We both could have been. They call me Dick. Yeah, not great, but it's because I'm always going on about my dictionary. The boys don't understand the whole word thing, but then that's just incomprehension.

The three of us will always be best mates. I like the idea of us propping up a corner of the bar when we're all in our seventies, telling everyone about everything we've seen going on around here. And all the girls get on well too, so they'll be there somewhere, watching us.

'Yeah Mate, right on to Jamaica Road.'

This cabbie's new. The rest know where to take me. I'm usually asleep in the back, but then most times it's about three in the morning. I'll be with my other half, Sandra, in five minutes and she has promised me, on the budgie's life, that she's gonna be ready. That bird should be in heaven relaxing on a sun lounger the times she does that and then takes two hours to get ready. Tonight, we're off to some new club and I've got a pass into the VIP area, so I'll bet a week's wages she'll be ready as soon as I get this fella to honk his horn.

I met Sandra when I was fourteen, at a holiday camp in Little Hampton. Don't worry; it wasn't one of those childhood sweetheart things. You know the sort where they write into late night radio shows with a love letter, telling the world and his wife about how they overcame their parent's disapproval to get married young, and how difficult it was with three kids by the time they were twenty-five. I hear it all the time on my headphones whilst I'm watching girls march out of Whispers, crying over some bloke, or telling their mates that so and so is a tosser. I don't see how any fella can go his whole life and only ever have been with one bird. As the letter's being read out and the DJ tells us how sweet it is that they're celebrating fifteen years of happiness, I'm thinking, darling there's no way some other woman hasn't fallen out of a club cursing your old man for breaking her heart.

So, that summer I spent a couple of weeks with Sandra and her mates having a laugh and trying to keep out of trouble. I didn't say much; I had a limited vocabulary in those days. Then, seven years later I bumped into her in a pub in the Old Kent Road and she'd moved to North London. I think she was impressed with how I'd developed; I told her she had exquisite skin. Of course, when it came to settling down she had to cross the river. You can't expect a man with the south in his blood to go north. Jack and Alfie would have never let me live it down.

'Mate. Take the second left after The Swan.'

Before we pull up, let me tell you about that bit of trouble with the suits earlier. I'm standing outside the bar; just a couple of minutes before Midnight and the cab pulls up. At the same time the suits decide it's time to go home and they fall through the doors. The big bloke walks right past me, bold as you like and goes to get into *my* cab. Well, I weren't gonna have that, after booking it, being prepared. I wasn't up for a fight, I didn't want any trouble. I'd finished work and anyway this bloke's rotten; all I'd have had to do was breath on him and he'd have been on the deck.

So I told him, real nice, 'Look mate, that's my cab. There's a cab office next door.'

He got brave and told me to get back to my ape job. He said that he would offer to share the cab with me but where he's going you need to be able to spell your name to get in.

He swayed, dribbling as he held on to the door of my cab. His little red bloodshot eyes looked at me, like he was trying to take me on.

Like I said, I didn't want any trouble; I'm not a violent person. I just figured it was time for one of my words. I walked up to him and shoved him, very gently, away from the car.

I said to him, 'Look mate, don't push it. I'm irrecusable.'

They said that word in a court programme on tele' the other day and I looked it up. It means "Not be challenged or rejected". Sorted!

What Maria Wants

'There's something living at the bottom of the garden.' Maria played with the curl that had escaped from her ponytail, as she spoke into the phone. 'Don't laugh. It's okay for you, living it up in that luxury hotel whilst I'm here with some kind of alien under the pear tree.'

'Firstly, I'm not living it up I'm working, and secondly this place is hardly what you would call luxury. I don't think it's been decorated since 1985. My room stinks of smoke.' There was a cheeky smile in Jake's voice that did nothing to cheer up Maria.

'Hmm. Well, if you come back and I'm not here I would have been sucked up in a space ship and they'll be doing awful experiments on me.'

'Okay, honey. Well just remember to pick up my grey suit before you go. I need it for next week. I've gotta run, the meeting's starting again. I only slipped out to tell you I love you.'

'Huh. But will you love me if they turn me green and take my brain?'

'I'd love you pink with blue spots. Gotta fly. Love ya.'

The phone clicked. She sat by it to see if he would call back and say goodbye again, like he used to. The silver phone, digital triplet to the one in the kitchen and the other in master bedroom stayed silent and so she rose from the sofa and drifted into the dining room. She should be doing something, making use of her time, but the pile of cardboard and other card-making paraphernalia held no appeal. She didn't fancy anything on television and she hadn't been able to read for weeks. This is how she became when the feelings got this strong. She needed Jake.

Later in bed, Maria tossed around, kicking the duvet off her legs. The room was stuffy, the central heating made the air thick and her throat dry. So far, this September had been full of warm days but cold nights. As she opened a window she caught sight of the dark silhouette of the paddling pool she had deflated a couple of hours ago. Jessica's giggles filled her ears, the image of the pink swimming costume with the cream frill, too big and baggy, and the little yellow armbands Maria had insisted the youngster wear in five inches of water, played in her mind's eye. She leaned out of the window, the straps of her flimsy nightdress hung over her shoulders. The howling noise had come from the very back of the garden. She knew it was foxes, but the child-like cries unnerved her. A light came on in next door's garden shed.

Bruce and Joan Butcher were in their sixties. They had lived in the cul-de-sac for forty years and were a mine of information on all the neighbours, past and present, alive and dead. They had welcomed Maria and Jake two years ago. Joan waltzed up the front path with a carrot cake in a Quality Street tin and a bunch of hand-picked flowers. She returned the next afternoon and sat with Maria eating the cake, drinking tea and relaying a potted history of the last owners of the house.

Maria could see a figure, that she assumed was Bruce, moving around in front of the shed window. Beyond the shed were dark fields and a small wood. The shapes of the trees were prominent against a deep blue-black sky. The cool air was refreshing, and she was starting to feel more relaxed.

'Bruce, will you hurry up and finish in there.' Joan's voice came from somewhere under the conservatory awning.

'Have your drink and go to bed. I'll be done when I'm done, woman.'

Maria laughed. The shed door opened and Bruce looked up at her window.

'Look what you've gone and done now. You've woken poor Maria. Sorry, love.' He waved.

'No. You didn't wake me; I was just getting some air.' Maria folded her arms over her chest, conscious of the thinness of her night clothes. Joan appeared in front of the conservatory and walked to fence, stepping through the flowerbed to rest her arms across the wood. Bruce joined her.

'Hello, love. Are you okay with Jake away?' Joan shouted up.

'Not bad. It's a bit quiet, but I'm fine.'

'Well, I know it's a bit late, but we're just going to have a hot drink if you want to pop in.' Joan turned to Bruce. 'She should pop in, shouldn't she?'

'Seeing as you've woken her up, she might as well.'

Maria could see Bruce's wide smile and watched him jump as Joan dug her elbow into his side.

'I think I might just do that. I'll see you in a minute.'

'Lovely.' Joan stepped back onto the lawn and headed for the house, undoubtedly to give it an unnecessary quick tidy.

Maria pulled on a pair of jersey tracksuit bottoms, a sloppy charcoal jumper and slipped on a pair of pumps. She threw a long cream cardigan over her shoulders, letting her untidy knot of curly blonde hair stay trapped in its collar, and trotted down the stairs. It was a bit crazy to be going for bedtime drinks with her neighbours, but she wanted the company and sleep wasn't coming any time soon.

The Butchers' living room was large but cosy. Soft light came from a tall lamp in the corner next to the bay window and two mock tiffany lamps at the other end of the room. Rosewood furniture, heavy with photographs and porcelain figurines, and a pair of dusty pink two-seater sofas and a matching armchair, filled most of the space. Bruce sat upright in the armchair whilst in the corner of one of the two-seaters sat a ball of wool with two knitting needles stuck into it. Maria settled into the remaining sofa.

Joan carried a tray into the room and placed it onto the coffee table. The three of them sat there blowing into steaming mugs. The sofa was comfortable. The high back invited Maria to rest her head and close her eyes. In contrast, the sofa in her living room was black leather and hard; the back too low to relax properly.

'Well, it's been a funny old week.' Joan spoke into the air above her.

'It's only Wednesday,' Bruce answered.

'It might only be Wednesday, that doesn't stop it being a funny week.' Joan sat forward and looked at Maria. 'Is Jake this argumentative?'

Maria smiled at them both. Jake wasn't argumentative at all. He didn't row. When they first met she found that a relief. There had been so many arguments and tears in the years before, she was grateful that he either agreed with her or told her what his view was, and that was that.

'Anyway,' Joan continued, 'I bumped into Gloria on my way to the shop on Monday morning.'

'How's the shop going?' Maria asked, not sure she wanted to hear more gossip about the neighbours. She bumped into Gloria herself now and then. The woman seemed nice enough. Every time Joan disclosed some titbit about someone, Maria found it hard to look them in the eye the next time she saw them.

'Not bad. We do a lot of trade for a charity shop. I sold three suits yesterday. St Mark's will do very nicely out of that.'

'Good for you.' Maria sipped at the bitter coffee.

'As I was saying; I saw Gloria. That woman has had so much to put up with. You just can't understand how it happens. People work hard to bring up their kids and then they go bad.'

Bruce coughed. Joan ignored him and carried on talking, leaning forward in her seat. 'Her eldest has gone and got himself into real trouble. Apparently, he and his friends have been stealing bottles of cider from the off-licence on the High Street. He got taken to the police station last Saturday and given a caution. That poor woman, what with her Chlöe having to move schools last year, she must wonder why she bothered having children at all.'

Maria winced, caught herself, and tried to smile at her neighbour.

'Children eh. I wouldn't want to be bringing up children in London these days.' Joan continued.

The heating started to make the room stifling. The recycled air made Maria cough. She apologised for the splutter, gently putting down her mug on a small portrait of one of the Butchers' young grandchildren, made into a coaster some years ago.

'I had better be getting off. Thanks for the drink.'

All three stood up and walked into the hallway. Bruce opened the door and put his arm around Maria's shoulders. His chest was warm and soft as he squeezed her into him.

'Well, you pop over any time you like. I'm always here even if Madam is single-handedly rebuilding St Mark's hospice.' He winked at her.

'Ignore him. I've done my shifts for this week, so I'll be here too. But your niece will be over, won't she? I saw you get the paddling pool out.' Joan smiled at her. Bruce raised his eyes to the ceiling.

'No, my sister can't make it.'

'Oh shame, I'd love to meet them. They never seem to quite make it over, do they?'

Maria exchanged pecks on the cheek with both of them and strolled across the paved drive that separated the houses. She turned and waved as she opened her front door.

The bedroom was cool. The window was still open and the breeze had blown the photograph of her and Jake, which had been propped up waiting to be framed, from the bedside cabinet onto the raspberry bed covers. They were both smiling, ski goggles reflecting the winter sun of Chamonix, holding up their ski passes for the camera. It had been their first trip after their honeymoon. Jake talked endlessly of the wonderful life that was stretched out before them. They could go anywhere, do anything, he said. What he meant was that now his ex-wife was looking after his children he was having a second youth, living a carefree existence, being spontaneous. She couldn't deny that they'd had a wonderful time. The group they skied with was fun and Jake had been perfect: attentive, tactile and loving, but she found the weight lifted from his shoulders, now become a gaping, jagged hole in her stomach.

The dark feelings descended again. It was late now, but she needed Jake. She reached for her mobile, typed a text saying she missed him and waited. She was pulling the covers back as a beep sounded from under the cushions and pillows. The display was still lit as she grabbed the phone and opened the message.

"Only a couple of days now. C U soon. Love U. Jx"

The morning light seeped through the slats of the venetian blinds and woke Maria. Giving up work to decide what she wanted to do had seemed like a fabulous opportunity, but this morning she craved routine. She ached just to pull on her blue and white pressed uniform, slip her feet into her comfy loafers and grab some toast before heading to the hospital. She missed the staff room, the moaning over lunch in the canteen, the busy ward. Jake had listened to her for months, as she described how hard nursing had become, how little the nurses were recognised or rewarded, until finally he suggested she give it up and find something else to do. They could afford it, and he wanted to see her happy, he said.

She walked to the wardrobe, pulling last night's jumper over her head, and tying her hair back into a messy knot. Her intention was to pull out her old uniforms, have another look, as a kind of test of whether she was doing the right thing, but as she moved clothes across the rail looking for the starched dresses, she found Jessica's coat. The cream padded jacket with fur around the hood took her breath away. She held it to her face, inhaling deeply. There was no smell. She panicked. Why couldn't she smell her daughter anymore? She wanted to smell her daughter.

The memories of that day rushed at her. Friday's had always been a race: for some reason the headmistress of the small Catholic school insisted the children finish fifteen minutes early, to start what the tall, serene woman called a weekend of family time. Those fifteen minutes were a nightmare for Maria; they made the journey along roads choked with traffic stressful. She always ended up running up the leafy drive to the two-storey building, looking for Jessica's face among the children carrying cardboard castles, papier-mâché angels or some other project.

That Friday, Maria pulled up the handbrake, grabbed her overflowing handbag and jumped out of the car. It was exactly two forty-five as she pressed the key fob and the indicator lights flashed on, the alarm set. A sea of children, clutching colourful pictures of sunflowers, to celebrate the feast day of St Julie, gushed into the playground. Maria spotted Jessica wearing her coat by the furry hood only.

'Mummy, look. I got a gold star for my sunflower.' Jessica ran to her and thrust the picture up towards her.

'It's beautiful, darling. Well done. We'll have to show Daddy.'

'Can we put it on the fridge?'

'Of course, if we can find space.'

'We can take some of the others down. They're baby pictures.'

Maria laughed. At six years old her daughter was already starting to discard things she thought were babyish.

Sister Brigid came towards them as Maria took the picture and Jessica's coat from her daughter. The woman moved slowly, her simple grey skirt swinging slightly as she walked. She placed a warm hand on Maria's shoulder.

'Hello, Mrs Buckley. How are you?'

'I'm very well thank you, Sister. How are you?'

'Very well. Jessica has been a little bit poorly today. She seems fine now, but she was a little quiet earlier and she had a rest in the prayer room. I don't think there's anything to worry about, but you might just keep an eye on her.'

'I prayed to Jesus and he made me feel better.' Jessica piped up from between the women.

'That's what he does.' Sister Brigid patted Jessica and nodded goodbye.

They drove away calmly. Jessica chatted from the back, playing with the Loopy Lou doll that lived in the car. Maria stopped at the supermarket, as she always did on a Friday. As they made their way through the aisles Jessica tugged on Maria's uniform.

'Mummy, I feel sick.'

'Really? Or do you just want us to stop shopping?' smiled Maria.

'No, I feel sick again and my head hurts.'

'Okay, well ten more minutes and we'll be finished and then you can go home and have another nap.'

'I'm going to pray to Jesus again.'

Maria hurried the rest of the shop and drove them home. Unusually Jessica didn't want a snack or to watch television. The girl let her mother change her into pyjamas and slip her into bed, without any fuss. When John came home to a silent house, he checked on his sleeping daughter before joining his wife for a peaceful evening.

At three o'clock in the morning Maria woke to the cries of her daughter. She pulled herself out of bed and walked to the next room, slipping under the covers and folding her daughter into her lap. Jessica's forehead was warm and clammy.

'Oh, you poor thing. It must be a bug.'

John came to the doorway.

'She's quite hot; will you get some Calpol for me?' Maria whispered to her husband.

Jessica drank the thick medicine and within twenty minutes was back asleep.

'She'll be fine in the morning.' John told Maria as she padded back into their bed.

At six o'clock that morning Maria woke again. This time the cries were louder, verging on screams. Jessica was holding her hands across her eyes. She said her head hurt and she was hot. When Maria pulled back the covers she froze at the sight of little purple spots across her daughter's arms.

'Get me a glass,' she shouted into the air.

John walked into the room, swaying with sleep.

'What?' he said.

'Get me a fucking glass.'

'Calm down, what's wrong?' He looked at his daughter's arm in his wife's hands and ran from the bedroom. Jessica started to cry in big heaving movements.

'It's okay, baby. Mummy's here. You're going to be fine.' Maria started to cry.

She prayed to Jesus, God and all the saints that the spots would disappear from her daughter's skin under the pressure of the glass, but they didn't. It took them only minutes to bundle the child into some clothes, dress themselves and get into the car. The only sounds on the journey were Jessica's sobs and the kisses Maria planted on the girl's head.

At ten o'clock in the morning, three days later, Jessica died. Maria and John made it through the days that followed and the funeral, supported by family and friends that stayed on rota. For a year, the couple mourned together. They kept the painfully small grave bright with flowers, the picture of the yellow sunflower laminated and bound to the headstone. On the first anniversary, after a memorial mass and a quiet meal with their families, John began to talk about what he called "starting again".

'Maybe we should move house, Maria.' He took the last of the plates from the dining table and headed for the kitchen. She waited for him in silence. He came back and put his lips to the top of her head. 'And maybe we should think about having another child. We're both still young enough.'

Maria started to cry. 'You know I can never have another child. I can never risk losing another child.' She looked down at her lap, at the screwed up tissue she had been kneading since lunch.

'You feel like that now, but it might help. We could never replace Jessica, but we could be a family again. We're both only thirty-two; we've got a lot of life in front of us.'

'We've got a lot of years to get through, you mean.' She stood and walked out of the room.

They went on for another year. John tried to get her to look forward, but she couldn't. When she looked at him she saw Jessica and that would only allow her to look back. It was Maria who left one Saturday morning, as John cried, telling her he couldn't live in the darkness any more, that he couldn't accept a life without any hope.

Maria threw herself into her work at the hospital. She was nearly herself there, helping others, being relied upon. She had never expected to meet anyone else, but Jake had come along, bruised from a divorce. He was desperate to be a good father to the two children he was leaving behind, but determined not be the kind of man that had two families. He never wanted more children and it suited her. His ex-wife was determined that Maria wouldn't be a second mother to the boys, demanding that her contact was minimal. It all seemed perfect. No guilt for not giving Jake children, no need to play happy families, and she got someone to care for her.

Now, as Maria stood in front of her wardrobe and finally let go of Jessica's coat, she told herself it was her state of mind blocking out the smell and that it hadn't faded, not yet. There were weeks, no months when she thought she was moving forward; and then there were days like this when the air felt so heavy she had to fight to move.

She showered, allowing herself a few tears and dressed in jeans and a pale blue mohair jersey. As she tidied the house, putting away her abandoned arts and crafts material, the doorbell rang.

Joan stood at the door wearing a navy skirt with a white short sleeved blouse, and her hair blow dried into neat waves. 'Hello, love, just popped over to make sure you're okay and see if you'd like to join us for dinner this evening.'

'I'm fine thanks, Joan. Thank you for the invite, but I think I might just have a lazy night tonight.'

'Okay. Well we're only next door if you need us.' She turned to go and then stopped. 'Oh, and another thing; I don't mean to overreact, but I've heard that Gloria's Matt was arrested last night. Apparently, they stole cigarettes and whiskey from the Spar. Just make sure you lock up – you never know where it might end.'

Maria thanked her and closed the door. As she walked back into the dining room, the phone rang.

'Hello there. How are you this morning? Still missing me?' Jake's voice was bright.

She tried to mirror his mood: 'Yes. And are you missing me or just enjoying the mini bar?'

'Now, I've told you about difficult questions in the morning.'

She laughed, but she wanted to tell him that she needed him home right now. She wanted to tell him she couldn't stop thinking about her daughter. She wanted to tell him that sometimes when he was away she inflated the paddling pool, pretending her niece was coming, but really it was to be able to see those clear images of Jessica again. She wanted to tell him there were days when she drove around with the Loopy Lou doll in the passenger seat, next to her. Most of all she wanted to tell him she was ready to care for a baby again, but she knew that wasn't the woman he had married.

'I've been thinking,' Jake said. 'I was talking to one of the blokes here. He's just come back from a trip to the Serengeti. Do

30

you fancy it?'

'Sure. It sounds great.' Her tone did not match the words.

'Don't be too enthusiastic.'

'Sorry. It sounds amazing. I'm just missing you.'

'I miss you too. So let's have a look on-line at the weekend and book it. It'll be stunning.'

She sat on the step in the hall once the call was finished. Her legs felt heavy and nausea was creeping over her. She needed fresh air and to be active. Another day stuck in this house would kill her.

The garage hadn't been cleared out since they moved in and even then they had both brought boxes of 'stuff' with them that hadn't been sorted for years. She threw out the easy things, half full tins of paint, cheap garden chairs that they never sat on, and rolls of loft insulation that they had over ordered. What was left, apart from tools, were four or five big crates and boxes, the contents of most she had no idea about. There was one huge black crate which she had looked in before. The first time in years, was about six months ago. It contained Jessica's things: toys and clothes, and the books that she had been learning to read. Maria's mother had said it might be best to keep only one or two things as keep-sakes, but Maria couldn't do it. It felt like abandonment. She imagined Jessica looking down from heaven, disappointed in her for letting everything go. So, there was this crate and everything else was in storage on an annual charge.

She stood with her fingers resting on the hard black surface. Nothing would be any better if she looked inside again today, nothing would be resolved within her; it never was. Moments passed and she stayed perfectly still, deep in thought, remembering her little girl. When she could stand it no longer she rushed from the garage, slamming the door shut, and into the house. She grabbed her car keys and handbag, and climbed into her car.

Maria drove for two hours. She didn't know where she was going until she spotted the sign for the shopping centre. She pulled into a space on the third floor of the multi-storey car park. Her hands shook as she pulled down the mirror in the sun-visor and looked at her face. She saw her mother look back at her, deep-set eyes and the beginnings of grey hair around the temples. The engine quietened as she turned the key and stepped out into the cool, dimly lit concrete space. She needed to be alone, yet surrounded by people. This seemed like a good place.

A nondescript tune played out softly as she walked into the centre. Large tubs of plastic foliage, surrounded by wooden seating dotted the concourses. People sat holding bags of shopping on their laps, or squeezed between their ankles. They looked at her as she passed them, but none of them knew her or acknowledged her. Her mood started to lift as she ambled about, carried along by the throng of shoppers. At a make-up counter, she even allowed a woman, wearing too much mascara and perfume, to try a new face cream on her. The place was busy. The top floor cafeterias had queues at each station. She joined one selling baked potatoes and ate her first decent meal since Jake had been away. Full, she continued to browse. The shoe shop had a sale. She tried on a pair of soft leather mocha boots. They fit perfectly, rising over her calf and stopping just below her knee. She paid a girl called Maxine sixty pounds, smiling broadly as she accepted the big bag.

As she strode through the galleries of shops looking at clothes and bags in the windows, her breath felt like it was coursing more freely through her lungs than it had for days. She wanted another coffee and more to eat. The escalators went from the second floor straight back up to the fourth, a huge stretch of metal that missed a whole level. As she looked around at the shops she was missing on the journey, a sign hit her. "Sale – everything you need for baby - 20% off." She turned to look at the top of the escalator, making out the umbrellas of a juice stand. The moving stairway delivered her, but she couldn't stop. She walked past the juice stand and the crepe hut to the lifts. The doors opened and she squeezed in, not pressing any buttons, letting Fate decide where she would get out. When the bell pinged and the third floor stood before her, she walked out onto it.

The shop was quiet, despite the sale. Aisles were full of baby paraphernalia: feeding bottles, warming devices, potties and hard plastic bibs. Shop assistants moved around, fixing sale signs to the merchandise.

'Can I help you?' a large girl with frizzy red hair asked.

'Just looking at the moment, thanks.' Maria smiled.

The girl looked at Maria's flat stomach and walked away. It annoyed Maria.

Maria followed the redhead to the other end of the store and started to look at prams and cots. The girl did nothing. It was like she knew there would be no sale. Like she knew that there would be no baby. Maria started to rock one of the prams. The girl turned briefly and then continued stacking a shelf.

'Excuse me,' Maria called out.

'Yes.'

'I'm looking for a car seat.'

The girl rose from her knees, making the sound of a much older woman, and joined Maria by a raised platform covered in car seats.

'How old is the baby?' the girl asked.

'Six weeks.' The words came out of Maria's mouth without her thinking about it. She had started to do stuff like this: tell strangers at bus stops that she was off to pick up her little girl, ask shop assistants if they had clothes in size six, walk around with them and then dump them just before she left the shop. She'd never done it this way; pretended Jessica was a baby. But it was this girl's fault, she shouldn't have looked at her the way she did.

The redhead had just rearranged the car seats. There were five pulled to the front of the platform.

'These ones in the front are all the ones suitable for new-borns. Then it's about how long you want to be able to use it and whether you want it to go with a pram system. Is it a present?'

Maria looked at the girl for a couple of seconds. 'No, it's for me, for my daughter.'

'Lovely. Well you look super for having a baby six weeks ago. You must have been fit before.'

Maria bent down and swung a cream coloured car seat around. A picture of Winnie the Pooh was stitched onto the belt. The girl bent down and joined her.

'That one's lovely, but it only goes up to six months, although they do it all by weight. How much does your baby weigh now?'

Maria tried to think. Jessica has been seven pounds, two

33

ounces when she was born. What would she have weighed at six weeks? 'Twelve pounds.'

'What's that in kilograms? They only have kilograms on these seats.'

Maria ignored her; she wouldn't let the girl catch her out. She touched the merchandise spread out in front of her, looking at each one carefully. The girl was still talking to her, but Maria wasn't concentrating on the words; she just nodded and uttered the occasional 'yes'.

'I'll take this one.' Maria pointed to the Winnie the Pooh car seat.

'Okay. Do you want me to order one, or do you want to take one today?'

'Today.'

'Let me just go and get one from the back.'

By the time the girl had returned with a plastic covered car seat, Maria had chosen other items: bottles, nappies, milk.

'Is there anyone helping you with this lot?' The girl asked as she took Maria's money.

'No, I'll be fine. I've got my car.'

'You'll never carry all this. Give me a minute; I'll get some cover and give you a hand.'

The girl shouted to her friend before Maria could object, picked up the car seat and headed for the exit. The girl took long strides, negotiating the crowds skilfully and reaching the entrance to the car park quickly.

'Right, lead the way.' The girl let Maria pass.

They got to the car and loaded the goods into the boot.

'So is dad doing his first babysitting duty?'

'Sorry?' Maria asked sharply.

The girl blushed. 'Erm, I was just wondering who was looking after the baby. It's none of my business though.'

'Exactly.'

Maria watched the girl walk away, her red hair hung across the back of her white uniform. She turned and gave a tentative wave before she disappeared around the corner. The boot of the Audi was full and the car seat lay on the floor, a little brown bear only just visible under the plastic. The shakes returned to her hands as she fitted the seat, getting her hands caught in the seat belt and cursing as a finger nail split painfully. When everything was buckled in or stored, she headed back into the shopping centre. She still needed more coffee. She still needed more food.

The shopping centre was slowing down. Maria found a seat at the coffee and bun hut easily and was served quickly. The café mocha was sweet, the foam and chocolate shavings stuck to her upper lip and the smell made her sigh. A tired looking woman manoeuvred a bright orange pram in between the seats and sat at the table next to her, ordering a fresh orange juice. A small whimper came from inside the felt-covered carriage. Maria watched as the woman gently rocked the pram and the sound stopped.

'Sorry Madam, we're out of fresh orange juice.' The waiter chewed gum as he spoke to the woman. 'There's a juice hut just over there.'

'I can't be bothered to move. Have you got any apple juice?'

The waiter nodded and disappeared. Maria was relieved; she wanted the woman to sit there. She wanted to hear the baby again.

'I know how you feel. Once you find somewhere to sit, that's it, isn't it?' Maria smiled.

'Absolutely. I'm knackered. But it's been good to get out.' The woman was younger than Maria, maybe twenty-five.

'Boy or girl?' Maria asked, pulling her chair closer to the woman.

'A girl. Bethany.' The woman raised herself in her chair and looked into the pram.

Maria watched a smile spread across the woman's face. 'May I?' she asked as she stood to look in the pram.

'Yeah. She's just about asleep. We're very lucky. She's very good.'

Maria beamed into the pram and then sat back down.

They chatted as they drank; Maria told her about her own little girl, at home with her dad. When they finished the woman started to walk towards the toilets. Maria followed her.

'Goes straight through me,' Maria said as the woman noticed her. She held the door as the mother moved the pram through into the toilets and tried the door marked disabled. It was locked.

'Oh, what a nightmare,' the woman said. 'I'll have to try

35

another one.'

'Well, I'll stay here and keep an eye on the baby if you like.'

The woman hesitated for a minute, looking Maria straight in the eyes.

'Okay, if you don't mind. I'll only be a minute.'

'That's fine. I've had to do this myself.'

The woman, put her baby bag on top of the pram, stroked the child's face and went into the cubicle.

Maria was sweating as she pushed the pram through the doors of the shopping centre and into the car park. The shoppers had been like obstacles as she weaved through the crowd, not daring to look over her shoulder. The concourses had seemed more narrow; the benches and rubbish bins bigger and greater in number. When she reached her car, she lifted the baby from the pram kissing the soft pink face and placed it gently into the car seat. Her fingers scratched at the steering console as she slotted the keys into the ignition and started the engine.

The CD of soft chill-out music started to play again as Maria parked as close to her front door as she could manage. The car seat came out of the car easily, much more easily than she remembered with Jessica. She was grateful for the emptiness in front of the Butchers' house as she let herself in and carried the sleeping baby into her dining room. The tiny buddle felt warm and smelt of talcum powder as she lifted her out and held her, stroking the baby's face against her own. She wanted to go into the garden, but she needed time to figure out what to say to Joan and Bruce. It would be okay once she figured it out; they would be happy for her. Jake would be happy too, once he understood.

The baby took the milk without any fuss. This was a good sign. Maria changed her and watched her fall back to sleep. As she carried the baby upstairs the door bell rang. She ignored it carrying on up towards the bedroom. The bell rang again. Maria laid the baby on the bed and then sat at the top of the stairs. She could see Joan's silhouette through the frosted glass. The bell rang again.

'Maria, are you there, love?' Joan shouted through the letter box.

'Maria. There's police at the top of the road. Blue lights and everything. You should come and see this love, I reckon it's Gloria's Matt again.'

Maria stood up, walked to the bedroom, picked up the baby and looked out towards the bottom of the garden.

Say Something

'Stop. Stay. Say something!'

Simon stooped, staring sideways.

Sighing, Sarah said, 'She's stolen something; she's surreptitiously stolen souls.'

Sarah stood. Should she show Simon salty streams? Should she surrender? Show some softness?

'Simon,' she sighed softly, 'surely *she* seduced?' Silence.........

Simon shivered, seemingly struggling.

Sitting, Sarah slowly sipped Sancerre; staring, studying Simon's surface; seeking safety, salvation.

Simon sat swiftly, showing sorrow. Sounding small, Simon said, 'Sarah, she's sexy, sensuous....'

'She's Satan!' Sarah spat. 'Spiteful! Shameless!'

Simon staggered, stepping slowly, seeing Sarah's sadness. She'd screamed Saturday, she'd screamed Sunday. She'd sat stroking sentimental stuff. She'd smashed Simon's saxophone, supposedly settling scores.

Simon suggested she settled, stopped screaming, saw sense.

She stopped, saw sense, screamed silently, stood. She scooped suitcases, shot scornful stares, set-off.

Simon smiled, satisfied...

Lamé Belts and Cardboard Crowns

I was fourteen years old when I first saw Rick not being Rick, and I was five when I first met Rick being Rick. He was my forever-in-black, forever-smelling-of-strong-coffee drama club teacher. I thought he was posh, but in hindsight he just pronounced his aitches in the right places. He had the most incredibly malleable face; a contortionist of lips and nose.

It must have been quite a sight for my mum the first time I went to drama, watching the back of seven-year-old Wayne Childs take me by my tiny hand and walk me down the street to the theatre club at the end of the road. That had been the end of my shyness and the start of what my father later called, 'a singing-dancing-nightmare'.

I can't remember too much about those early days. Later, we played a warm up exercise, where everyone had to say the word cabbage using different emotions. I wanted to unleash the hidden character in me like Fiona, an ex-dancer from Staines, said we should. I prepared to find some cool American bubble-gum chewing kid, or maybe a mad old woman. I waited patiently as cabbage went around the circle. Kids were shouting, or whispering. Joanne, a delicate pretty girl with satin chestnut hair, looked down at the floor and then quietly, almost inaudibly, mumbled the word. As soon as she finished she looked up and beamed at us all.

'I did shy,' she told us. We all clapped.

Cabbage was only two people away from me. I squeezed my hands into fists at my side, and tried to feel Rick's theatrical energy pumping through my body. Finally, it was my turn. I dropped to my knees, pulled at my hair, then tugged at my t-

41

shirt. Then, I threw my arms above me, spread my fingers wide, raised my eyes to heaven and declared.

'S P I N A C H.'

'Hmm wrong vegetable, but what were you trying to convey anyway,' Fiona asked over the laughing.

'I'm not sure. Maybe happiness?'

'Happiness,' Joanne giggled. 'I thought someone had nicked your bike.'

Rick rubbed my back and said, 'Great emotion, Becky.'

As we packed away, Rick came over to me.

'You need to store away what you felt today. Be ready to pull it out when someone gives you the right lines. It was good.'

I stacked the last chair and left the hall, lighter.

That was the same year I played a river. The play was called 'Development Blurp'. I got to sit for two hours covered in blue plastic, waving my hands up and down and making gurgling noises. My mother was horrified at the end of the first night.

'She could suffocate,' she told Rick backstage. 'It's dangerous, all that sheeting.'

'She's fine. Didn't you see we cut out a hole for her head? She can breathe okay.'

What they should have been worried about was the tricky manoeuvre I had to do at curtain call. Hours under hot lights made me sweat even without the artistic arm waving. The bottom of the plastic got wet and slippery through the show and standing up to waddle to the front was no mean feat. On the second night, out of my mother's gaze, I did slip and crashed into Bradley Harris who was wearing a pair of his Dad's old trousers tied up with thick string, and a waistcoat Rick had found in the props trunk. Bradley had a real speaking part, the farmer who was polluting the river. As he bowed and the audience booed, I attempted to walk up behind him to take my bow. Instead I whizzed into him and ended up grabbing the string. His mother said the rope burn lasted for several weeks.

When I was ten years old Rick called me into the tiny office-cum-dressing-room at the back of the church hall that doubled as our drama club. He cleared the chair opposite him of lamé belts and cardboard crowns and pointed to it. I sat down, resisting the urge to spin in the leather chair that reminded me of Master Mind. He looked at me for a long time; his thick eye lashes fixed open, and his high cheek bones raised as he smiled.

'Now, Becky, I want to talk to you about the next production.' He picked up a dainty tea cup and saucer. My nan had a set just like it. The edges of the cup were frilly with a gold line around the rim. I could smell the strong coffee as he drank.

'We're going to do a short run at the Young Vic, exciting eh!'

I nodded. He was buttering me up, I could tell. I didn't want to be a tree or a shepherd.

'This is going to be very special. People will be watching.'

I hoped so.

He put down the cup and pulled my chair towards him.

'We're going to do a play called, "The Princess with a Load on Her Mind". It's by a man called Wilfred Harvey. It's a great play.'

'What's it about?' I asked, before I thought.

'Well. Erm. It's about a Princess who is worried about something.'

'Right.'

'The thing is there are lots of parts in the play. Servants and the King's men; all sorts.'

Here we go, I thought. I'm going to be a throne. I'll be plonked on the middle of the stage and everyone will sit on me.

'And the really exciting thing is that I want you to be the Princess. I think you're ready. You were such a convincing river last year.'

'Really, you want me to be the Princess?' I stopped and thought. 'Rick?'

'Yes.'

'Does the princess actually come on to the stage? She's not sick or anything and just shouts from the wings?'

Rick laughed. He had a crumb of something stuck in his beard. It shot forward and landed at my feet.

'Yes Becky, the princess is actually on the stage. In fact she is in every single scene. What do you think to that?'

I jumped off the chair and into his lap.

'Thank you, thank you, and thank you. I am going to be the best Princess Waterloo has ever seen. I am going to practice

43

every day. I'll only eat steak and caviar until opening night. I'll learn to walk with my back straight and my head held high. I'll stop biting my nails. Yes, I'll definitely stop biting my nails.'

Rick turned his chair so that we were both facing the mirror that ran the length of the wall. He flicked a switch under the dressing table. A square of light bulbs flashed on, giving the room a stark white light.

'Now, young lady, this is going to be your season. We'll get your costume made. It will need to be something regal, something in gold.' He held the lamé belt across my chest. 'And we'll design your make up.' His fingers drew circles on my cheeks.

'Oh my mum will make my costume. She'll make as many as you like.' I stood up and kissed him. 'Thanks Rick.'

I think I floated home that Saturday afternoon. My mother wasn't as enthusiastic about making the costumes as I thought she would be, but she did it.

Rick was still Rick that summer. He put us through our paces as we learnt our lines. It turned out that the Princess was a liar, although my mother convinced Rick to change the script to fibber, who spent most of the play in the centre of the stage in bed. It was a step up from plastic sheeting, and I had the most lines, so I was ecstatic. Only the final scene worried me; the Princess's fibs were exposed and the King put her across his knee. As the lights went down, the final sound the audience would hear was the sound of the King smacking his daughter's bottom. David Costello, the butcher's son, played the King. In rehearsals he did as Rick directed, and as we pretended the lights were dimming he clapped his hands hard to mimic the slap and I let out a wonderful cry. But David, a big boy who was a couple of years older than me, was always up to something.

'I'm gonna smack your arse proper,' he taunted as we walked home the night before we opened. 'I'm gonna make sure it stings and there's nothing you can do about it.'

He was sweating. Fiona had made us finish up with one of her dance exercises. His pale blue t-shirt had dark patches under the arms and across his back.

'I'll tell Rick.'

'Tell who you like.'

I could feel my bottom lip start to tremble as I looked at him. My eyes focused on the knees of his gray trousers, which were dusty from the hall floor.

'Only joking,' he laughed as he ran across the road and into his Dad's shop.

I sweated as much as he had for the next twenty-four hours. My mother put my quietness down to nerves, as she tried and re-tried my costume on me, uncertain as to whether the tiara she had made out of an alice-band and diamante studs was regal enough.

Just when I thought I was going to die of fear, it was time to go to the theatre and get on with it. The dressing rooms were full of kids in gold, silver and red; faces painted in garish colours, crowns and soldiers helmets askew and plastic swords zooming through the air in play fights. Rick hushed us all and then called David and me to join him in the wings.

'Look at the front row,' he told us, as we peeked through the gap in the curtains. 'Those two sitting there at the end. They're from the paper. They're going to do a review. Give it your best shot. Break a leg.'

David and I looked at each other, nodded and went back to the dressing room in silence.

The show started. The place was packed. With the lights up, I couldn't see anyone, but I played my heart out to the front row. The audience clapped in all the right places, and laughed when they were meant to. At the interval Rick and Fiona congratulated us all on a faultless first half.

I had almost forgotten the torture of the last day as the second half whizzed by. I projected my voice, watching my diction, and exaggerated my movements just as directed. When the final scene came, I bent across the King's lap. The lights went out and he hit me.

We had to wait three days for the review to appear in the local newspaper. Rick pinned it up on our notice board.

"Downriver's production of 'A Princess', provides a wonderful introduction to children's theatre. The performances are full of humour. The lively cast carry Harvey's play along with energy, especially Becky Wilkins in the lead

role, who portrayed the cheeky Princess with gusto. The final scene is funny and moving, and one could almost believe that the wayward girl was being smacked for real as the curtain closed and her screams echoed through the auditorium."

The next summer Rick decided we were ready for Shakespeare and, as I had demonstrated I was prepared to suffer for my art, I thought I might just be in line for the role of Titania. I was to learn an actresses' life is not an easy one. The week we started reading the play a new group of kids joined. There were five of them, all from Islington. I can't remember how they heard about our little club, but they came along and changed everything. The girls, all a couple of years older than us, wore short skirts and make-up. Our boys went silly for them. Ruth was the oldest and prettiest, she quickly claimed Nicky Beavan, a thirteen year old boy with floppy blond hair and a bed that came out of the wall. Every time you turned round they were snogging, and as the roles were announced, art imitated life and Ruth was cast as the fairy princess to Nicky's Bottom. I did okay, I got Puck, but it wasn't the lead.

The play stretched us all. We struggled with the language, and Rick struggled to direct us when we didn't understand what we were saying.

'I can't get my head around this stuff.' Nicky held a hand to his brow. 'How am I supposed to learn these lines when I can't even pronounce the names.'

'What names are you struggling with?' Rick stood up and moved into the middle of the circle we had formed.

'Pyri –something and Fizz-something.'

'Pyramis and Thisbe.' Rick sat crossed legged in the middle of us. 'This isn't easy, but you are all capable. Once the penny drops you will love it. I promise.

Nicky made a face and shrugged his shoulders.

'Right enough reading for today. Boys, can you go with Fiona, she's going to do some improvisation with you. Girls, we're going to work on getting inside the mind of Shakespeare's women.'

The boys marched out towards the stairs to the creepy crypt; our second rehearsal space. The girls put away the chairs and sat on the floor waiting for instruction. We did some warm up exercises and then Rick talked us through how to feel like women of Athens and fairies. I was to ignore that Puck was a man; we were using poetic license. Rick made us glide around the hall, moving our limbs elegantly, swinging our hips and trying to float. We followed him in a line; making whooshing noises as we breathed deeply, pretending we could smell the aromas of a forest. Rick loved it. He skipped about, flicking imaginary hair, and drawing on lips with his fingers. At four o'clock, he called time.

'Stay in character girls,' he cooed at us. 'Pick up your bags like debutantes and drift home.' He waved liked the Queen as we all moved out of the hall.

The run went well, not as well as 'Princess', but then Sheila, Nicky's mum, was supposed to make all the costumes which she confessed she hadn't done two weeks before the show, and most of us went on wearing bed sheets. There were no journalists this time and so Rick wrote a review himself. He picked out each character, giving praise and finally saluted the whole cast as a magnificent ensemble.

At school, life was tough for me. I was sinking in a sea of a thousand pupils in the huge comprehensive, stuck in the unseen middle; no A student, but too bright to need special attention. I was desperate for a merit mark, something to prove that I turned up. Rick spotted it; a few weeks after Midsummer Night's Dream had closed and my new term had started, he asked me to help him catalogue the few costumes we had worn.

'Why so blue Becky?' he asked, as I tucked Titania's cape into a suit bag.

'No reason.'

'Oh come on. You can't fool old Rick.' He pulled one his faces. His lips collapsed inwards like a man with no teeth.

'I'm no good at anything at school. I hate maths and geography's boring.'

'You just need to find your thing.'

'Maybe.' I tried to smile but tears threaten to escape.

'Now stop that right now.' He took the suit bag from my hands and hung it in a silver wardrobe. 'What homework have you got this week?'

I told him about the pyjama case I had to make for needlework and the project I was working on for history. He screwed up his face.

'What else?'

'I have to write something about how people work together for General Studies.'

Rick lit up. He disappeared from the room and returned a minute and a half later with his review.

'What better example,' he sang as he smiled at me, took a sheet of paper from the desk and started to write.

We worked together on an essay for hours. Rick prompted me to remember how we had helped each other to learn our lines and how we had run around to everyone's houses getting spare bed linen.

I handed the piece in with a smile, and received it back with an even bigger one. I got my first A and my first merit mark.

Two summers went by; I was fourteen years old and sure that I was just perfect for the part of Mum in "Ernie's Incredible Illucinations." The reading was about to start. We were all in the hall, stretching and breathing with Fiona, hoping that Rick would arrive soon and we wouldn't have to do star jumps. We heard the big church doors open and close and waited for Rick to appear. As I heard him walk down the corridor, I expected the vision in black to appear; but what came into the room was a bright purple dress, the hem clinging to American tan tights smoothed over prickly legs. For a moment, I thought it was an extreme new exercise.

Rick walked differently. He kind of hobble-swayed over towards us as he pulled a chair behind him. He motioned for us to sit on the floor. We moved closer and gathered around him in silence. Fiona stepped to the back of the hall. She had one hand on her chest and the other on a hip. She tilted her head to one side and nodded to Rick as he sat with his hands on his knees. Rick spoke slowly and calmly; he told us that today was the beginning of his new life; Rick was in the past and Rosemary was his future. He pulled one of his faces and then clapped his hands.

'Right, on with the reading. Best voices you lot. Parts awarded by the end of the day.' His voice cracked.

We were all young teenagers but none of us laughed. We were transfixed. I could still see Rick through the caked foundation and ruby lips, but I could see Rosemary too. I don't remember my parents' reaction. Rosemary continued to teach us for a few more months and then one day she wasn't there and Fiona introduced us to Greg who was a pain in the arse drama student from Henley. Within a year the school closed, and although we all tried another one most of us gave up and concentrated on being hormone fuelled horrible teenagers.

And now I am stood here outside of this church; my heels slipping on the rough gravel. It was Joanne who called me and said I just had to come. She said that we all owed him, that he had taught us all that we had talent and that we could be anything that we wanted to be. She's a journalist now, writing features on education for one of the broadsheets; not bad for a girl who at twelve years old had to be convinced by Rick, that school still had more to teach her.

'What if I hadn't listened to him? I'd have been pushing a pram by the time I was sixteen. I wouldn't have this life.' She had begged down the phone. 'And Nicky's coming. He's taking a day off from lobbying, for whatever he's lobbying for these days. Think about what he taught you.'

I put down the phone after making a tentative promise. Joanne's final words echoed around me. Two days later, I booked the day off work and bought something suitable to wear.

And now, after kissing people that I haven't seen in a decade and holding back tears I didn't know were there, I have figured out what to tell Joanne. Rick is the reason that I can recite Puck's speech to Titania, but Rosemary is why I always look beyond the make-up.

The Accident

It was a month after the accident when I finally went to the doctors. Anne had been on at me, and despite trying, I couldn't rise from the armchair without huffing and panting the way my grandfather used to.

'Why are you being so stubborn?' she said, as she dusted around me. 'Why do you have to do this to me?'

'What am I doing? I'm just sitting in my chair, reading a newspaper and trying to keep out of the way.' I tried to lean forward to reach my cup of coffee without grimacing.

'You're sending me to an early grave with worry, that's what you're doing. Why won't you let me make an appointment? It's alright for you, sat there. I'm the one not sleeping, worried out of my mind about you.'

In fact, sleep wasn't that easy for me. If I lay on my back, my neck felt like it was supporting a hundred-weight of head and if I laid on my side the muscles across the top of my shoulders went into spasm. And, whichever way I arranged myself, Anne's throaty snores kept me awake.

I should have seen the bike, not only because then I wouldn't have to do these exercises and wear this awful orange coloured brace, but because SHE was beautiful. I was working from home, staring over the screen of my laptop, watching the grey squirrels running around in the garden. And I was trying to be green, not printing out the fifty page report that needed my final review and sign-off. The constant swapping of reading glasses and distance glasses was making me feel old. The door of my study opened onto the patio. Late September sunlight shone into the room and added to my difficulty in reading, by throwing a glare across the screen. I wanted a cigarette. Sod it, Anne was out for the day, the garden was warm and at fifty-five years old I was big enough to smoke if I wanted to. I had my slippers on and my head full of thoughts of deep inhalations, when SHE hit me.

When I opened my eyes SHE was standing over me; a short jean skirt stretched across her thighs and a frilly top hung loose over her chest.

'My God. Are you alright? I'm so sorry. I thought you saw me.' SHE held out delicate hands, the finger nails painted a soft pink, towards me.

I pulled myself up, doing a little jump as I stood to show her I was okay. The doctor said later, that wasn't a good idea.

'No harm done. I thought you were going into the road,' I said boldly; lying. 'More to the point, are you okay?'

There was a trickle of blood on the inside of her ankle. I took a handkerchief from my pocket, concealed the embroidered DM, bent down and wiped it. SHE didn't flinch. SHE let me do it. I felt a tiny twinge in my back as I stood and smiled at her, poking the bloody square of cotton back into my pocket. Her eyes were bright and young; no need for the heavy make-up, the thick gothic black lines that so many girls her age wore. SHE smiled at me.

And now, Anne is not smiling. She is counting out multi-coloured tablets into a plastic cup, telling me that I wouldn't have needed so many if I had gone to the surgery when she told me to. She hands me the cup and another filled with purified tap water. She stands and watches as I force them down, one after another, the sugary coating making me feel sick. When I hand both cups back empty, she stacks them and sits down on the sofa opposite me. I try to see her thirty years ago when we met. She was a pretty girl; long milk white legs and a tiny waist. But she was in a rush from the start: rushing to make us a couple, to get engaged, to get married, to start a family.

'I don't know what you're so scared of,' she said one night as we walked home from the cinema, her hand wrapped in mine, jammed into my coat pocket. 'I love you and you love me; getting married won't change anything.'

We had been together for a year, although we'd known each other for longer. I liked her, I might even have loved her by then, but I didn't think we needed to get married, not at that point. I was working for a bank, making good money, enjoying the lifestyle and happy to have a great looking girlfriend like Anne; marriage could wait. A month later it was taken out of my hands. She told me she was pregnant as we walked along by the Thames, headed for a couple of drinks at The Red Lion. In panic I told her I'd marry her and she leapt at me, winding those legs around me, kissing me from forehead to chin. It was too late a week later when she realised it was just a scare; I had said the words and I couldn't take them back.

'Do you feel any better, David?' Anne smiles with her head to one side as she talks to me. 'You've almost finished the yellow tablets. Has any of the pain gone?'

'Yes. My lower back feels less tight. It's just my shoulders and this arm.' I tap the bandage and screw up my face.

Anne puts her hands on her knees and stands up. I watch her move out of the room, straightening out the latest family picture as she passes the bookcase. The cast of my family look down at me: our two sons, their wives and the three grandchildren. The boys laughed when they heard about the accident, their wives were more concerned and the kids sent handmade cards. They will all come here now this Christmas, because I can't drive and none of them want a day without some festive spirit; we will all stay together under this roof. Anne thinks I have ruined it, although she doesn't say so. This year was supposed to be different. This year we were supposed to be going to Mike and Roslyn's. This year the kids were supposed to be looking after us.

Anne comes back into the room and sits on the sofa again. The light streams in from the big bay window behind her and catches in the waves of her hair, which is darker now, the grey hidden. She is wearing a pair of navy trousers, and a cream top which sinks into the fold between her breasts and her belly. There is no news in the paper Anne has bought me. They had run out of anything decent and I am skipping through a tabloid comic surreptitiously turning back to page three, the only thing of any interest. I can't help but keep glancing at my wife as she struggles with a crossword. She takes up more of the sofa than SHE did.

I blushed when SHE noticed the rip in my trousers that gaped, showing a swathe of white boxer shorts.

'Oh gosh I should pay for that. It was totally my fault,' SHE muttered, putting her hands to the perfect skin of her face.

'Nonsense. It was a bad call on my part. You were on the cycle lane. You had right of way.' I laughed as I tried to pull the jagged pieces of material together. 'If anything, I should pay for any damage to your bike.'

We both looked at the silver bicycle. There was a small scratch on the wheel arch. I took out the handkerchief again, spat on it and rubbed at the metallic paint work. 'Damn. Definitely a scratch. Why don't you come inside?' I pointed to my front door. 'I can see to it now.'

'There's no need. It hardly shows.' SHE smiled again. Her teeth were perfectly straight inside her rose coloured mouth.

'I'd feel much better if you let me see to it. And I don't know about you, I could do with a drink.'

SHE followed me inside and waited in the hall as I pushed the bike into the garden and then went upstairs to change. My shoulders hurt as I raised each leg into a new pair of trousers. Back downstairs, I poured us both a small brandy and showed her into the living room. SHE sat in the middle of the sofa, pulling her skirt down over her thighs with one hand and cradling the cut crystal glass with the other. I was amazed at how much SHE had done in her twenty-four years. It spilled out of her. It's amazing how much people open up when you listen. There had been a year travelling with her boyfriend, but he had stayed in Australia. Then there was work at numerous companies as a freelance graphics designer and now there was a big break; a job designing TV credits for a production company. SHE sat further back in the seat and relaxed. I supposed SHE felt safe, with the photos and my reassurance that my wife would be home soon. And, I supposed my fifty-five years helped.

It had been five years since my last affair; a short interlude with a woman I met in a car park in Crewe. She needed directions and after ten minutes of trying to explain how she needed to weave through the city centre streets, I had ended up walking her to an appointment. The affair had lasted as long as my business in the area. She seemed relieved when I ended it, and I felt nothing. It was my fiftieth birthday the next week and my taste in women hadn't changed over the years; I still fancied the ones with the smooth faces, the flat stomachs and the boundless energy. But, I had no desire to end up a sad old man, or to be spurned, and so I stopped. Anne had never suspected. She had everything she ever wanted and everything she needed. I stopped before I failed.

SHE finished her drink and joined me in the garden as I fixed up the bike. SHE called me clever for disguising the scratch with silver paint, and for a moment I thought SHE was going to kiss me. 'If she moves any closer, I will stroke her face,' I told myself; 'If she wants this, I will let it happen one last time.'

I watched her blow at the paint to encourage it to dry, helping to hold wispy strands of her hair away from the wet shine. I imagined feeling that same hair spread across my chest, stroking it as SHE slept. My hands started to sweat and my wedding ring spun easily around my finger.

Moments later, outside the front door, I watched her raise her leg as SHE climbed onto the bike. A glimpse of pink knickers made my breath catch, and then SHE was gone.

'Pop in again if you're passing,' I called into the afternoon.

Anne looks up from her quiz book and asks me if I want tea. I nod and she rises again. She stands at the doorway and looks at me.

'I'm taking you back to the doctor if you're not a lot better in a week,' she says.

'I'm fine, Anne.'

'Well at least one good thing has come from all this.' She walks towards me and sits on the arm of the chair. 'It was time you gave up work anyway. You've worked long hours all of our married life. Once you're better we'll be able to get on with our retirement. Just you and me.' She kisses my head and then stands and goes to the door again.

'Oh and when you're done can you make sure you pop that paper into the bin beside you. You might be suffering, but there's no need to make a mess.'

I take one last look at page three, fold the paper, throw it into the bin, and close my eyes.

Open Me

The tin had a label on it. It read, "Open Me". Shirley put it to one side, again. She had hoped clearing her aunt's attic would give her the chance to find hidden treasures or family secrets, buried for generations. She didn't like the bold invitation; it spoiled the feel of her covert mission.

The light was fading outside; it was after five o'clock in November, even in the windowless attic she knew it had to be getting dark. The day had been unseasonably mild and bright, but now a chill crept under her pashmina, and caught the exposed skin between the top of her jeans and her thin wool jumper. She rose to a stooped position and carefully made her way to the open trap door, pulling a large cardboard box along with her. The descent was tricky. A fall wouldn't be clever, no-one knew she was here tonight and images of her lying in a broken heap flashed into her mind's eye. She made her way gingerly down the ladder, resting the box on her shoulder and head until she felt the floor beneath her feet.

The rug in the lounge was vivid against the faded furniture. It sprawled out in front of the electric fire like a sticky pool of blood, dark red and thick. Shirley sat down on it and started to sort through the box, putting the little "Open Me" tin to one side. A stack of black and white photographs with lacy cream borders were on the top. She recognised her mother as a child in several, in every one holding her aunt's hand and looking up at her. There was a big age gap between the two sisters, over twelve years. Her mother blamed the difference in years for the women not being close, that and the fact Sissy had failed to support her when she had wanted to get married young and her father had tried to stop her. 'But then what would a dedicated spinster know about love', Shirley's mother had told her. There were only a few pictures of Sissy on her own. In one she sat on a garden chair, looking thoughtful. She wore a half smile, which could have been a half grimace. There was a table to the side of her, two glasses were visible and what looked like the edge of a cake. Shirley turned the picture over hoping for some clue on the back, but it was blank.

A bang made her jump. She rose to her feet and moved through the hall and toward the kitchen, following the echo of the noise. The kitchen was empty, her mother and father had spent the day clearing it out, putting things into different boxes which her mother had labelled useful and useless. Shirley checked the floor and under the only remaining piece of furniture, a large pine table, to see if anything had fallen. Nothing. A tiny wave of paranoia made her check the back door and the windows. They were still locked. The key to the kitchen door hung on a small hook the other side of the room.

Back in the lounge she continued to rummage through the box. There were two champagne corks with coins stuck into them; strange keepsakes for a woman who never seemed to celebrate. Sissy had come to them every Christmas for dinner; one of only a few times year she joined the family. She always brought small practical presents, with the receipts tucked into an envelope in case anyone felt they needed something else. Her aunt would arrive wrapped up in a thick coat, long scarf and a hat, at midday on the dot and leave at five in the afternoon, thanking them for their hospitality as though she was visiting the home of a distant acquaintance rather than her only sister. Her mother gave a sigh of relief as Aunt Sissy left, her duty over for another year. 'Now Shirley, aren't you thankful that you don't have a sister to put up with?', her mother usually sang as the latch on the garden gate caught. Shirley wasn't thankful. She hadn't celebrated being an only child, even if it meant undivided attention and more affluence than her friends with multiple siblings.

Next, Shirley lifted a large piece of paper from the box,

bringing it in front of her face. As she started to read it, it was blown from her fingers and floated through the air to the other side of the rug. She wet a finger and held it up, attempting to register a breeze. She could feel nothing except her forehead work its way into a confused frown. 'Now I'm getting spooked,' she said to herself as she retrieved the paper. It was a certificate; an award from Rosemary Robert's School of Dance, dated 1948. The edges had curled, but the design of two dancers bent gracefully, was still bright. It was awarded to Cecily Knox and William Butcher for third place in ballroom. Shirley couldn't imagine her aunt ever dancing, and especially not dancing with a man; she barely tolerated Shirley's father and rarely spoke to him directly in all the years Shirley could remember.

At Shirley's wedding, her aunt had refused to dance or even socialise with anyone. The woman had sat at a table alone, despite Shirley bringing friends over to try and keep her company. It had been embarrassing. All Sissy had done to each reluctant visitor was smile weakly and look sideways, past the dance floor, towards the exit. Eventually, Shirley had given up and when her mother said, 'Just let the miserable woman get on with it,' Shirley agreed to ignore Sissy and enjoy her evening. No-one noticed her aunt leave, but later her father confessed to ordering a taxi and helping her to slip away.

Shirley tried to think of when she had ever seen her aunt happy; when she had seen her laugh, or even smile. The truth was that it had been rare. Whenever Shirley had been in Sissy's company, it had made her sombre; even as a little girl.

As Shirley delved into the box again her mobile phone rang, making her gasp. She checked the number and then breathed into the mouthpiece.

'Hi,' she whispered.

The voice on the other end was her husband; the clear line delivered his voice from Barcelona as plainly as if he were sitting next to her. He told her she sounded odd and distracted and then launched into a description of his hotel room and an account of his meeting with the Spanish suppliers. She half listened, still pouring through the box, as he described the man he didn't trust, with whom he had to sign the deal to make his trip worth it.

'Not my money, so I'll do it 'cos Frank really wants this deal,' he told her. 'But trust's important Shirl, and I just don't get a warm feeling with this one.'

She didn't have a warm feeling either. The temperature in the room seemed to have dropped dramatically in the last ten minutes and she was cold but reluctant to light the ancient electric fire.

'You there?' her husband called.

'Yep sorry, I'm here.'

'Well I had better go. Why don't you go and jump in a nice warm bath? Miss you.'

'Miss you too.'

The silence after she pressed the little red button on the phone was heavy. She had lost her appetite for treasure hunting and started to pack up the box. She'd pop it in the back of the car and look again tomorrow. As she closed the cardboard flaps she remembered the "Open Me" tin. It wasn't on the rug where she could have sworn she had placed it, nor was it on the sofa behind her where she had put the champagne corks as she was looting the box.

'I must be going barmy. It couldn't just disappear'.

The kitchen light was still on as she retraced her steps. The table and the worktops were still empty, but the back door was open wide. A few spots of rain spattered the linoleum and a scattering of leaves had blown inside. Shirley rushed and closed the door. She shook her head as she noticed the silver key in the lock and the empty hook the other side of the room. She turned the key in the door and pressed her face up against the small pane of glass. The darkness outside was now heavy and complete, the rain on the glass distorted the vague hints of shape she could just make out. Her heart raced and she recited an internal mantra of calm as she wrapped her pashmina around herself tightly. The light in the hallway burst on as she flicked the switch and dashed back into the lounge, searching for her handbag with her car keys in it. The mantra was turning into a silent plea that she would be okay, that she was just freaked out. Her breath came in quick spurts as she wished that Ben was at home waiting for her instead of in that hotel room, inevitably raiding the mini bar. She now did mean it when she told herself she missed him.

Her bag was on the empty sideboard. She whipped it up, threw it over her shoulder, and then bent down to pick up the box. As she lifted it a glimmer of silver caught her eye. It was the "Open Me" tin, sitting proudly on the rug. Shirley felt herself linger, swinging the box towards the sofa and then back square in front of her body, as she tried to decide whether to take the tin or beat a hasty retreat. Finally, she threw the "Open Me" tin into the box. As she moved towards the front door she heard keys turn in the lock. A lump in her throat threatened to turn into a sob, she hoped a sob of relief as she imagined her parents coming to undertake their own after-hours raid. The front door closed and she waited, box pressed against her stomach and bag slipping down her arm.

'Oh my God!' The box fell to the floor, landing squarely with a thud, its contents still inside. 'Jesus, Oh Jesus!'

Her aunt stood in the doorway, a scarlet dress with a dainty ruffle around the neck visible under a lavish black wool coat.

'Don't be afraid. I just came back for a few bits, but it seems I might be too late.' The woman moved to the sideboard and placed a set of keys on the surface as she bent to open the bottom drawer.

'But you're...' Shirley shook her head and closed her eyes. She had to be ill. She had been working too hard, and sleeping too little. She slowly opened her eyes. Her aunt stood before her, looking at her.

'We had the funeral, you're dead.' Shirley shivered as she said the words, feeling scared and sick.

'Do I look dead?'

Shirley shook her head. Her aunt looked very much alive. Her hair was smooth and shiny; she was wearing a little make-up, something Shirley never seen before. And the clothes, the vibrant clothes looked foreign, yet they suited her.

'We've got rid of everything. We all thought...'

'It doesn't matter. I don't need any of this stuff where I'm going. I just wanted to take one thing and I can't remember for the life of me where I put it.' Sissy smiled.

Shirley put down her bag. She wanted to hug her aunt, but she never had before and now the gap between the women felt too wide.

'What are you looking for?' Shirley's voice shook.

Her aunt continued to look in the cupboard. She bent effortlessly, as she swept her hand inside the empty piece of furniture.

'I'm looking for a tin; a little tin.' Her aunt continued opening drawers and then moved to a little cupboard the other side of the room. Shirley reached into the box and took out the "Open Me" tin. She walked towards her aunt and was about to tap her on the shoulder when the woman, dressed in the most gorgeous scarlet, turned around.

'Ahh, that's it.' Her aunt looked at the tin, but didn't take it.

'I don't understand,' Shirley said. 'Your bag, it was by the river. And then they found you. Mum went with the police. She recognised you, she identified you.' Shirley began to cry.

'No disrespect, but your mother hasn't recognised me for fifty years.'

Shirley sat on the floor before her legs could buckle. She held the tin on her lap.

'Open it,' her aunt's voice said from above her. 'Go on, open it.'

Shirley lifted the lid. There was a single colour photograph inside. A smiling Sissy stood proudly in the centre, behind her a man wearing some kind of military uniform, smiled over her shoulder, wrapping one arm around her waist. They were both holding champagne glasses, sending a toast to whoever was taking the photograph. To the side of them was a table with a large cake. The icing read 'Engaged' and there was a miniature American flag. On the other side you could just make out a small girl, only half facing the camera. She had her face pushed into her balled up fists.

'My engagement and the day before our mother died.' Her aunt's voice was a whisper. Shirley kept her head down to hide her tears and stared at the photograph.

'You stayed to look after my mother.' Still she couldn't look up at her aunt.

'I loved her. She was my world.'

The voice was distant. Shirley finally looked up to find the room empty.

'I am going to be happy now.' The voice came from the kitchen.

Shirley looked again at the photograph in her hands. An icy chill blew into the room, and then she saw it, the scarlet dress with the delicate ruffle around the neck.

No Beep

The girl on the till kept doing it, but there was no beep. She looked at me and I looked at her, and we both raised our shoulders. She tried with something else; still there was no beep. The man behind me puffed loudly, sending warm air into my collar. I took two steps forward, out of his line of breath.

It was almost nine o'clock on Monday night. All-night supermarket opening brought the freedom to shop whenever you wanted or needed to, and the chance to beat the crowds. Tonight, I didn't want any crowds. I wanted to slip in, do my thing and slip out. It just wasn't working out that way.

The girl started to tap at buttons on the little pad in front of her. They did beep; a little high pitched computer song that gathered pace as she pressed randomly.

'One more go,' she said to me, pulling her lips hard across her face so that her mouth turned into a dark purple line.

She slowly and carefully picked up a box of cereal, located the little black bar code and showed it to the scanner as though she were holding up the name of a competition winner to a television camera. Still, there was no beep.

The man behind me continued to puff as he moved his Evening Standard between armpits and shuffled forward two steps. He brushed against my arm as he bent his head over the conveyor belt and looked at the periscope shaped gadget that was meant to register shopping items.

'What's wrong with it?' he asked.

'I don't know,' Chantermorelle answered him. Her name badge struggled to hold all the letters that spelt out her first name. 'It worked a minute ago.'

65

He looked at me as if my bag of fragrant basmati, which Chantermorelle had tried to put through several times, had caused the malfunction.

I contemplated picking everything up and moving to the only other till open, but it felt like Chantermorelle and I were in this together.

The minute hand on the large clock at the front of the store moved with a jolt. Time was against me. I had less than an hour to get home, shower, choose something casual to wear, apply a little natural make-up, and wait for *him* to pop in and find me hanging around, just watching a bit of television.

The puffing-man tapped his watch and sighed dramatically.

'I'll put on my light,' Chantermorelle said in response, as she reached forward to the little sliver switch in front of her. The three of us and the other people in the queue looked heavenwards as a cube with a number nine on it lit up above our heads. 'And I'll ring my bell,' she added.

A woman at the back picked her basket up from the floor and huffed. 'Oh come on. I'm on a meter,' she shouted.

No one responded. The woman turned on her heel and dashed off.

'Sorry,' Chantermorelle grimaced at the remaining queue. She sat back in her chair and started playing with her fingers. The nails were long thin works of art, painted vivid colours with stones in the thumb and ring finger. I wanted to ask how on earth she kept them so perfect working on a till. My own manicures, which I had been having every week since I'd met Tom a month ago, were always chipped by Wednesday. I was just about to make some small talk when puffing-man banged into me as he took his jacket off.

'So why isn't the manager coming?' he asked, as he tried to drag his arm out of a sleeve.

'I don't know. They normally come quickly.' Chantermorelle smoothed a thumb over her nails.

The man dumped his jacket on top of my shopping and looked at me as he breathed loudly through his nose, his nostrils widening to show a little unattractive nose hair. I held back a wretch as I thought about how I could have been at home preparing to pretend to be surprised by a wonderful man, and instead was stuck looking at the should-be-recipient of a personal hair trimmer.

With her nails now well examined, Chantermorelle patted her hair. It was piled up in an ornate bun, straightened afro hair smoothed down, with little red-tipped flicks sticking out at the top. She pinched the little peaks and twisted them, bringing them back to attention.

A tall teenage boy, fourth in our line looked down the queue. He didn't have a basket; he balanced two loaves of bread, a pint of milk and a bottle of bleach in his arms.

'Your mum will wonder where you've got to,' I called, without thinking.

'Piss off,' he barked, out of the corner of his mouth, dumped his items on the sweet rack and walked out.

Chantermorelle raised her eyebrows at me and shrugged. Her large gold hoop earrings bounced off the side of her head. I shifted in the small space between the bar of my shopping trolley and puffing-man. My movement brought him back to life.

'Why doesn't *she* help?' he asked Chantermorelle, pointing at a woman in the stores uniform sat at the information desk.

'I don't know,' Chantermorelle rubbed her fingers over both of her earrings in unison. 'She doesn't normally work in Customer Info; she normally does help.'

This time he took an enormous lung full of breath, drawing himself up and out so that he had the chest of a soldier. He finally let the breath out all over me, giving me the same look my father had when I'd failed my A'levels.

The light around us changed; the little amber cube's light had extinguished.

'Don't tell me; that doesn't normally happen.' I laughed, smiling broadly at Chantermorelle and the puffing-man.

'I don't know.' More hair patting. 'I don't normally sit on this till. That thing's meant to stay on for ten minutes.' She hit the switch again and bathed us all in orange light.

I tapped my club card on the Perspex counter, full of wishful thinking that the second calling would be effective and soon the beeps would be restored. A woman behind puffing-man started to collect her few items from the very beginning of the conveyor belt. She threw them back into her basket and marched off, followed by a man in baggy jeans and a basket ball vest. He sucked at his teeth as he carried away his three tins of super malt.

'Just us then,' I said to puffing-man.

'Humph!'

As I crossed my arms and resolved to speak no further words to the miserable sod, a flustered looking blonde haired woman whizzed up to the foot of the till. She squeezed herself into the tiny gap behind Chantermorelle, and switched off the glowing number nine.

'What's wrong?' she snapped, pulling a large set of keys from her waist. The luminous green plastic coil stretched along the length of her arm.

'I don't know,' Chantermorelle was in a huff. She crossed her arms. 'The thing that beeps is broke.'

The blonde said nothing. She turned a key in the side of the little pad and pressed some buttons. The computer tune struck up, this time accompanied by a drum roll from the receipt dispenser. She pushed puffing-man's jacket to one side and picked up my bag of basmati.

'Careful. There's no need to push my clothes like that?' he spat at her.

She gave him a fleeting look and said, 'sorry sir,' quietly under her breath as she swung my rice under the scanner. A loud high pitch beep sounded. Chantermorrelle pulled a face, her pouty purple lips went down at the corners and her forehead scrunched into little lines.

'I don't know what you do to this thing,' the blonde said over her shoulder, as she disappeared away from the till.

The giant clock's hand juddered as the items on the belt started to make their way from black rubber, to the sloping sliver, and towards the carrier bags at the end. As the rush of items sped up I remembered what was under the celebrity magazine and prepared a bag to move the box into, as soon as it was out of the carnival-nail fingers. It seemed an age ago that I had come in and now, as long as the technology held out, I was almost done. I stood poised waiting for the magazine cover showing Kerry Katona and her 101 ways to lose baby fat to be lifted.

Chantermorelle reached for the glossy; she lifted it and took her time finding the row of black lines on the back. The puffing-man stared at the box. I moved my eyes sideways to look at him; his faint smile fell as he caught my glance.

Finally, she lifted the box. It felt like she was purposefully spinning it in her fingers reading the words, fetherlite, ultra-thin, sensitive. She twisted around to another gadget behind her and held the white plastic security tag to it. As she pulled the box away the tag stayed in place. She tried again, still the tag stayed in place.

'What's wrong with it?' I whispered.

'I don't know.' She flicked the number nine cube back on. 'It normally works.'

The Way Down

It was almost six o'clock in the morning as I watched the sun rise from the summit of Mount Kinabalu. The mountain top was almost flat; a few gentle inclines and milky white boulders broke the surface, and ditches and crevices dipped beneath it. Sharp light from the brightest dawn I had ever seen bounced around. The air was thin, fresh and cold. A few steps left you entertainingly breathless, but recovery was rapid and I watched people move in short spurts, like children at a birthday party playing musical statues. Just above me, a row of triumphant climbers stood on a wide precipice taking photographs. An imaginary rope kept them a safe distance from the edge.

I jostled for position among the photographers. Together we made sure we captured every view of the clouds parted over a coloured sky, and the reflected light on the small rest house below. When the snapping and whirring ceased I took in the view again, this time more slowly and more purely without the glass lens.

'Come on Al, let's start to make our way down. We don't want to get stuck behind any of this lot.' Tony picked up both of our bags and stood behind me, holding padded pink straps for me to put my arms through. His eyes were slightly puffy; the part of his face that peeked from the gap between his cap and his scarf looked red and angered by the wind. I let him slip the pack onto my back and adjust it on my shoulders.

'This place is so amazing. It looks like a land of dreams.' I almost said it out loud, but instead sighed.

Tony stopped fiddling, stood in front of me and looked into my eyes. His expression was still and gave me no clue to what he was thinking. I hoped he was feeling the magic of the mountain the way I was.

'Tony,' I breathed deeply and looked straight into him. 'What do you wish for? What do you wish for right this minute?'

He held me by my shoulders, a gesture which had become a habit since we had moved from friends to lovers.

'You want me to be honest?'

'Yes, absolutely.' I was losing my feeling of romance and wishing I hadn't asked.

'What I wish for right now,' he paused.

I could have jumped in and provocatively put my finger to his lips, telling him I didn't need to hear the words, but I let him go on.

'What I really wish for right now is a poxy helicopter to get me off this mountain.'

I half-smiled.

We had arrived at the guide hut at the bottom of Mount Kinabalu early the morning before. The hut smelt of wet forest, Deep Heat and somehow damp dog. A thin threadbare strip of green carpet ran the length of the log room; a catwalk for parading expensive and highly sophisticated equipment. Everywhere, people checked maps, read the articles of previous climbers posted on the walls (including several stories about lost parties), examined the contents of plastic covered first aid kits, and waxed suitably worn walking boots with anxious seriousness.

Tony and I leant on the counter, pouring over a timetable and route map with a group of walking guides. They lavished attention upon us, running around to find us leaflets and helping us to understand the colour coded routes.

'So the main trail is straight forward. We just follow the yellow signs?' Tony reached across and put some coins in the guides' tip box.

'Yes. But you shouldn't worry. Azrul will be your guide and he knows the mountain very well.'

'Brilliant.'

Tony turned and shook hands with our guide, swallowing the man's fingers, palm, wrist and even some of his arm in his huge handshake. Azrul smiled at us, and then shook my hand.

'This is gonna be fantastic Al. You get to climb your

mountain.'

I laughed at how Tony gave me the mountain; my first present.

Azrul picked up our bags, effortlessly throwing one over each shoulder, and moved out of the hut. At the bottom of the mountain he returned our bags to us and unfolded a large map, waiting until Tony had finished drinking from his water flask before speaking. 'We will start from stair. You tell me when you tired. We will stop until you get more energy.'

Azrul stood on the first step of the climb, with Tony and I looking up at the ferns and flowers he described. Before we moved off he reached up on tip-toes to free Tony's collar trapped under the strap of his backpack.

'You have comfy today.' He smiled broadly, brilliant teeth inside a mocha mouth, and waved us butler-like to the beginning of our ascent.

Tony's call for a helicopter echoed around my mind, but the jubilation I felt at having attacked the mountain the day before and marched energetically up it, had stayed with me and I ignored the comment. I tucked my camera away in a pocket and followed Tony and Azrul to the path which would take us back down.

The first hour of the descent was fun. It was reasonably even ground and the three of us walked in a line with Tony and our guide finding the vocabulary to talk about Manchester United. I rushed to the exotic foliage I had missed on the way up and brought it back to Azrul, giving him little mysteries he needed to explain. He took each one and spread it across the palm of his hand before telling us its origin, or its story.

Soon things became more difficult as the descent became steep. Rocks jutted out of the red earth, and heels that had gone before us left scrape marks in the mud. Tall trees clung to the dramatic drops and smoking swirls of mist rose and tangled around them. I started to find the sharp smell of eucalyptus and crushed leaves overpowering.

'This is harder than going up.' I stopped on a ledge of mud, covered with the blood like heads of tiny red flowers.

'No way. Come on Al, I thought you said you were fit.' Tony

charged past me, jumping on to a large angular rock and balancing on it.

'I am fit Tony. I did really well yesterday. I'm just saying that it's hard on your legs when they're tired.'

'This was your idea babe and the sooner we get down, the sooner we can get ready, and the sooner we can get in the bar.' He jumped from the rock, continuing downwards. 'Maybe you should go to the gym a bit more, like your mate Lucy.' His words floated over his shoulder, accelerated, and smacked me in the face.

I walked behind him, wanting to put my hands round his neck and squeeze. I had been so proud of myself. I'd climbed 4000 metres of rugged mountain without a complaint, and he couldn't acknowledge that this was difficult. It was him who wanted the helicopter, him who had puffed and panted as we reached the summit, and him who had scared Azrul by displaying symptoms of altitude sickness fifty metres from the top.

'Tony!' The tears rose to the edge of my voice. 'Can you wait for me, please?'

I stood on the edge of a shelf of rock and wood. It was a slippery drop to the next level and I struggled to see where I was supposed to put my feet. Large fan shaped leaves hung over me, dripping moisture and slapping me as the wind blew them. A wet, narrow path wound off to the left lower down and disappeared under a shelter of trees. Tony stood looking away from me, just before the canopy. Twisted roots and chunks of stone lay below me. It was hard to believe that I had practically skipped up them the day before, and that we had stood and kissed as Azrul took our photograph in the spot where Tony now picked at layers of flint.

'Tony, please I'm scared. I can't get down this step.'

The sharp slopes and ninety degree angled turns reminded me of a petrifying theme park slide. I swayed.

'Tony! Can you hear me?'

He was about twenty feet away. The wind must have taken my words upwards away from him and back towards the peak of Kinabalu.

Azrul was at my shoulder, where he had been for the past fifteen minutes or so. He silently tried to mediate by taking my rucksack and trying to ease my descent. I smiled into his big deep brown eyes as he tried to coax me down from the ledge. I wanted to jump the way Tony had, but the signals from my brain were jammed in my belly and I couldn't activate my legs. Azrul tapped his own backside, suggesting I wiggle down on my bottom. A haze of embarrassment, frustration and pride surrounded me and I couldn't sit down on the floor of the path. He took my hand. Apart from the introduction in the guide hut, this was the first time he had touched me. I waited for him to try and make me jump, but instead he led me away from the edge to the side of the path where he pointed out a little clump of blue-ish mushrooms, growing under a thick tree. I bent down to inspect the oddly coloured fungus before starting to stand again.

'No. You not see flower good. You stay more.'

'But what about Tony?'

'No problem. I get Tony. Bad he no see flower.'

A thin stream trickled along the ground. I let my fingers rest in the water and felt the tension running out of their tips. The coolness seemed to bring back the firmness to my legs. I stood and walked towards the ledge, sat down and dangled myself over. The very tips of my toes touched the next level. The Gods shone on me as I took a leap of faith and landed squarely and solidly two or three feet lower down.

Tony and Azrul's voices came towards me as I brushed dirt from the back of my jeans. I was still scared of the trek to the bottom but I didn't want to let go of the success I'd experienced on this mountain. I couldn't let Tony, or this descent, hand me a bronze medal when I deserved to jump on the podium for the gold.

The two men were in front of me. They looked at me and we all stopped on the narrow track.

'I'm fine. Momentary blip.' I reached inside myself and pulled out the biggest smile I could find.

'Thank God for that. Maybe we can just get on with getting down now.' Tony turned and continued stomping over the path we had taken twenty four hours before.

Azrul placed a hand on the inside of my arm, just above my elbow, and held me all the way back down to the guide hut.

About the Author

T.A.Gilbert grew up among a tight knit community in Waterloo, South London. She was born in 1970, into a mixed race family; her father came to England from the Eastern Caribbean island of Dominica and her mother is a Londoner. She has been writing for as long as she can remember; she wrote a school play at nine years old and has always kept diaries, which sometimes make scary reading. It was a residential writing course, at Arvon's Lumb Bank Centre in the autumn of 2006, which encouraged her to start sharing her work.

Wednesday Night Tupperware is T.A.Gilbert's first collection of short stories. She looks forward to publishing her debut novel, 'Pushed', in 2009.

ACKNOWLEDGEMENTS

A massive thank you to Jan Williams, Hilary Gander, Cheryl Foreman and Lisha Gilbert. Also, thank you to the support of those in my two writing groups; a safe space to share is invaluable, as is the constructive feedback and the red wine. Thanks to Becky Crum for her ability 'to spin', Trevor Spooner for his constant requests for more reading, and Sharon Back for 'DEFENESTRATION'. Special thanks to Justine Solomans for those days in the British Library and the cocktails that followed.

Also, to Paul Magrs and Tiffany Murray; two fantastic writers who encouraged me to mimic no one, and keep going with my own style.

And finally, to Mum; yes it's finished now!

Printed in the United Kingdom by
Lightning Source UK Ltd., Milton Keynes
137536UK00002B/96/P

9 781849 232845